SHELTERED LIVES

Also by Frank Milburn

THE INTERLOPER

SHELTERED LIVES

FRANK MILBURN

Doubleday & Company, Inc.
Garden City, N.Y.
1986

Library of Congress Cataloging-in-Publication Data

Milburn, Frank, 1945–
Sheltered lives.

I. Title.
PS3563.I37157S5 1986   813'.54   86-6231
ISBN 0-385-19009-3

For Maria
And to the memory of
Marshall A. Best

October 1963

That first day at Fort Dix all the recruits had been marched down to the post barbershop for haircuts. David had noticed a thin soldier standing on line. The soldier had a full brown beard and hair that fell to the top of his shirt collar. The sergeants, directing and hustling the men, pointed him out and joked among themselves, but Allen seemed oblivious to them. His presence, however—for those few minutes when hundreds of young men made the actual transition from one world to another—lent the barbershop and its patrons the atmosphere of a soup kitchen. It had something to do with the comic way he held his cap at his side—exposed like a soft bowl—and the angle of his body, which inclined slightly toward the man in front of him.

"How old are you?" Allen asked. They were sitting in the crowded mess hall. He had come over and sat down at David's table. There had been something amusing about allowing their clothing to handle half the introduction.

"Twenty," David said.

Allen murmured something.

7

"I didn't catch that."

"I said, two years younger than me." Allen spoke softly; a pale unshaven face, yet one of intelligence and humor. "Where are you from?"

"Long Island," David said.

"Really?" Allen looked pleased. "Great. I'm from Flushing."

He continued eating; he looked scholarly as he bent over the tray, taking his time, thick rimless glasses a little down on his nose. Sergeants once or twice brushed by him, but he looked up at them innocently, his mouth full of food, conveying with a shrug that he was hurrying. David wondered if he had a stammer. Each word was formed so carefully, as if there were a chance it would get away from him. He noticed that Allen's hands helped to push the words.

"You were the one with the beard," David said. "At the barbershop."

"That's right," Allen nodded.

"Did you have any idea what would happen?"

"I thought it was wrong to shave it off the night before," Allen said quietly. "I don't know, I just thought it was wrong. Dishonest."

"You're going to have trouble from now on—with the sergeants, I mean."

"You don't approve?"

"Oh, it's okay." He was glad for Allen's company. "But I think it's tough enough without looking for trouble."

"That's true," Allen said with a smile. "It's tough enough."

It was not a good thing in the Army to be identifiable. Everything happened in twos and threes: in a sea of olive drab a sergeant's eye would latch on to the familiar face or name, and as often as not include in his glance the men closest to it. After the incident at the barbershop Allen had become highly identifiable.

He had something on his mind, but he did not confide in David, and David never pressed him. There was anger at the Army—"So much precious time," he would say bitterly, in that slow way he had of emphasizing each word—but it was more than that. Sometimes in the evenings David would watch him. While the other men spent all their time cleaning equipment, Allen took only a few minutes; then he would sit down on his footlocker with a book. He would read for a while but soon raise his eyes and gaze absently out across the barracks.

When the weekend passes were issued the problem was solved for a little while. Allen would leave on Saturday after inspection and return the following evening. Amid the noise of other soldiers returning, of equipment being cleaned and organized for the next day, of other voices and groups with their stories—those in khaki entertaining those in fatigues—Allen would move about the bunk, each detail important, describing concerts and clubs, a bookstore, an antique shop, some people in a park—David forgetting for the moment marching and rifles, Monday mornings and sergeants and standing at attention in the cold dawn air.

One Saturday there were no passes. The battalion commander pulled a surprise inspection: the men had twenty minutes to get all their equipment cleaned and laid out on their bunks.

David stood beside his footlocker and watched as the

battalion commander moved down the aisle. Beside him were the company commander, the first sergeant and assorted cadres all carrying clipboards.

Everything went well until the group reached a small nervous soldier by the bunk opposite David's, whose equipment was dirty, footlocker a mess, belt buckle tarnished, general orders forgotten. The battalion commander, a tall portly man with a soft voice, recited the defects as he moved around the bunk. "This man just hasn't *tried,*" he said, almost sadly. He moved on to David briefly, then toward the door. Going out, the battalion commander said, in a soft, almost deferential voice to the company commander, "I really don't think this barracks should get passes."

Sunday morning David and Allen, wearing their khaki uniforms, sat on the steps outside the barracks. It was a cool autumn day, bright and clear, and the company quadrangle looked almost pleasant—neat at least, as they surveyed it; dirt running track, border of yellow buildings, island of green grass in the center. They knew every inch of it from high-stepping runs around the track, from scooping up everything that didn't grow.

They sat on the barracks steps and Allen drew out a photograph and handed it to David. "This is Jane," he said. "We're going to be married."

Actually it was of both Allen and Jane together, clowning in some bright-walled kitchen. Allen was sitting on a table and she was feeding him a piece of cake; white frosting flecked his beard and shirt.

"She's beautiful," David said. "Who is she? What does she do?"

"She works in a bookstore and goes to NYU at night," Allen answered with a shrug.

"Is she from Flushing, too?"

"From the city," Allen said.

"When are you going to be married?"

Allen stood up. "I don't know yet." He stood beside David with his hands in his pockets. "We're trying to save some money."

David picked up the photograph from the steps and looked at it again.

Half of one Friday night they walked around a large parade field. The lights of the post flickered around them. Each time they drew near the regimental area Allen veered away. He walked with his hands shoved into the back pockets of his khaki trousers, kicking the grass in front of him.

"I'd marry her tomorrow," Allen said, "if I knew where the hell I was going to be for the next two years."

"Why don't you wait until you get your orders?"

"Because I've waited ever since high school. Anyway, I don't see what difference it would make even if we did get married. There're a lot of places overseas where I could take her. Germany, Japan."

David waited for Allen to once more, as he had done for the past two hours, balance the scale.

"Of course, one or two places I couldn't take her."

"Korea," David said. "And now Vietnam, I guess."

Allen stood for a moment, lost in thought, absently scuffing the grass with his shoe. "Christ, I don't know. It's a big step."

He took it. It hurt David a little when he wasn't invited to the wedding. It made him feel like someone casual: Allen's friend, yes, but not the closest of friends.

The orders were posted on the bulletin board one week before graduation. David was to report to a special infantry school at Fort Stewart, Georgia, near Savannah, for more advanced training; Allen was to remain at Fort Dix to train as a radio operator.

David was pleased: Georgia and Fort Stewart would mean the roughest kind of training. More important, he would have what he craved most: exhaustion. Exhaustion meant no past and no future; nothing but the physical present, nothing to think about except the job.

He knew all about Fort Stewart. It was the second largest military post in the country; a place where many of the Army's elite Special Forces slogged through millions of acres of swampland. It was the perfect spot to explore the longitudes and latitudes of exhaustion. It would also—no doubt— give him an opportunity in the course of things to confront one-on-one his substantial apprehension about snakes. That was the only part of the gung-ho training film running through his mind that gave him pause.

Allen, for his part, was delighted with his orders. Fort Dix was only two hours from New York, there would be weekends at home, a continuation rather than an interruption of his life. The Army was a pain, but Fort Dix was not the worst of all possible worlds for a draftee.

They pushed through the crowd at the bulletin board and walked up the road to the telephone booths where Allen could call his wife. David felt Allen watching him. When he saluted a passing officer's car, and another behind it, Allen said: "We'll have to make an effort to keep in touch. It's just too easy for people to get separated. You'll probably be glad to talk to someone. All you have to do is call."

"Same goes for you," David said. "But I'll only handle problems of a military nature."

Allen smiled. "I think my problems are all taken care of."

It suddenly occurred to David that, the Army being what is was, he might never see Allen again.

After he received his orders for Vietnam David called Allen from Fort Stewart.

"I guess this is what you wanted, Davey," Allen said.

"I guess so."

"You sound depressed."

"Oh, I'm not," David said. "I might as well put this training to use."

"You should get a nice quiet job like mine."

"Somebody has to do the dirty work," David said. "The price of freedom being what it is."

"Did I detect a hint of humor?" Allen asked. "A touch of irony at long last?"

"Goodbye, Allen. Let me know when you get your orders."

But David felt desolate when he hung up after their conversation. He hadn't realized how much he depended on these weekly telephone calls. This was especially true whenever he got back from a few days of simulated jungle training, living with slugs—human and otherwise. It meant a lot to David to hear from Allen about this other, civilized world; a world that seemed to be growing more foreign every day. Fort Dix was

7

certainly not the epitome of civilization, but compared to Fort Stewart it sounded like paradise. Over the past weeks David had come to believe that were they let back into civilian life, many of his new colleagues would be in state prison.

And now, Vietnam; a completely new thing he was going to be facing all alone.

Two nights later. "Yes, yes," Allen said angrily. "It says the same thing right here. Go on, go on . . . Yeah, yeah, that too."

"God," David said. "I'm really sorry."

"There's been a fuck-up," Allen said. "I *can't* go. I just got married!"

Then silence at the other end of the line. It lasted until David said, "Allen, are you still there?"

"In shock, but still here."

"Have you told Jane yet?"

"No, no. I'll call her later. How long is this goddamn thing?"

"Twelve months."

"All of 1964. You realize that?"

"Yes."

There was silence for a few moments, then Allen said in a quiet voice, "You know, I'm glad you're going to be there. I'd hate to have to go through it alone."

Two weeks later. "Of all the ways to get there," Allen said, in despair, "we have to take a boat."

At that moment his duffel bag slipped from his grasp and plunged into the water. He and David leaned over the railing and watched the bubbles and spreading circles. They heard laughter from the snakelike lines of soldiers below, and commands from the naval officers on deck. Allen looked up: his hands were still grasping the phantom duffel bag, as if word had not been sent down to them. Then he turned away and stalked through the hatch and into the bowels of the ship.

The ship, the voyage, was a sobering experience even for David. As soon as they left the calm of the harbor—the soldiers on deck leaning over the guardrails, smiling, taking pictures, a military band playing, bystanders waving handkerchiefs—the airlock doors closed with a whoosh and clank. A few of the men who remained below got seasick. A young soldier walked the length and width of David and Allen's compartment, saying, "Moo, moo," and then, "We want water, we want water," until another soldier walked up to him and knocked him unconscious.

"It's this having no control," Allen said, his hand over his eyes as if the dirty canvas bunk above him were giving off light. "How long is this trip again?"

"Twenty-one days."

"I'll have to borrow some of your clothes." Allen raised himself on his elbow and looked down at David, who was sitting on the lowest of three tiered bunks. "Hey, you having any thoughts about this?"

David said, "Yes," he was. He had not realized it would be this bad. "I'm thinking that maybe the Army was a mistake."

Allen got a laugh out of that one.

Later in the morning the captain of the troop transport addressed the men over the loudspeaker. He was friendly about the ship's course, the estimated time of arrival, the fish they might see, but uncompromising about the ship's restricted areas and the staggering discomfort.

"Gentlemen," he said at the end, his voice rising, the loudspeaker crackling, "I must ask you to remember at all times: This is a ship of war."

As details for the voyage David and Allen were assigned to the butcher shop. Their main function was to remove frozen meat—on hooks or in heavy wire-bound crates—from the ship's enormous refrigerators and set it out to thaw.

There were only the butcher, a huge fat man, and David and Allen to do the work. Sometimes the butcher himself would need help with the meat, so for hours at a time David and Allen would trim fat, make hamburgers or cut steaks. It was necessary to coordinate their work with the pitch and roll of the ship so as to avoid slipping on the floor, which was coated with grease and blood.

Much of their time was spent hauling garbage cans full of waste meat and empty cartons up five flights of narrow stairs to the stern of the ship, where they threw it overboard. Downstairs the fat man would tell them stories about his thirty years in the Navy; about the famous generals and admirals to whom he had personally served special cuts of steak, and about the ship once during wartime when the refrigerators had broken down and the meat had spoiled. His stories helped to pass the time.

Each morning David and Allen were awakened at five o'clock to begin work. They worked until five in the evening, with two breaks during the day; one each in the morning and afternoon. There were more breaks when the butcher, his face doughy white from years belowdecks, decided to tell a story.

On their last morning aboard ship they stood at the railing near the stern. They had just thrown overboard a mixed assortment of garbage, and now it bobbed in front of them. The first light of dawn glinted off orange rinds and meat crates, milk cartons and hundreds of ice cream containers.

"It must have been quite a shock when you first got to the States," David said.

"You know, I hate this goddamn garbage detail."

"Sunrise and garbage," David said. "A good title for my memoirs about the war."

"I like it." Allen smiled.

"I'm going to miss all this," David announced with a weary sweep of his hand toward the horizon. Ice cream containers bounced in the golden wake of the ship. "I'll miss the pork chops and the veal cutlets, the liver and bacon and the shit on a shingle. My children and grandchildren won't believe how long everything took to defrost. Perhaps they'll believe me when I show them the actual wire cutter that snapped crates open like you'd snap the neck of an enemy soldier."

Allen laughed. "You know, you're getting real nasty. I like you better this way."

"I'm stealing the wire cutter," David said. "I want to show it to my grandkids and see their faces light up. They'll probably want to know how I got frostbite when the temperature outdoors was 97 degrees."

Allen leaned over the guardrail and looked at the churning white foam below. In a few minutes the trail of garbage disappeared.

"The first day I got there," Allen said quietly, "right off the boat, my family went to my cousin's place. I was about twelve years old. The first thing I asked my cousin was what time it was all right to take a shower. You see, over there it would take time to get the wood, and make a fire and everything. But he said, Go ahead, anytime, and that was the first time it came through to me that I was really in the United States."

Allen turned around and leaned with his back against the guardrail. "The next thing—the same day—was the television. I'd never seen one before, but I'd heard about them, and knew there were people in America who had televisions. My cousin had one and I asked him to turn it on. I'd been in the country about two hours, but that's what I wanted to see. So I sat down, ready for anything, and the picture came on and the first word on the screen was WAR, in big block letters. I watched it for about ten minutes, and there was only that one word. It was about the only word in English I knew, and I kept expecting something to happen; there'd be a bulletin or something. I was really excited: here I am, my first day in America, and we're going to war."

"So what happened?" David asked.

Allen shrugged. "It was this station's call letters—in New York. WOR. My English spelling wasn't so good."

They could make out land now.

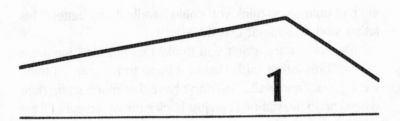

January 1965

They were near the house and the driveway was white, with only a dimly outlined set of tire tracks left by his father when he had gone to the airport earlier that morning. Branches, heavy with snow, hung down to a man's height across the road.

The driveway was a quarter mile long and near the end took a turn, climbed a steep hill, then opened onto the house. David could feel the silence outside. He remembered the driveway as a child on winter days like this—he and his sister and perhaps a friend or two clutching the frozen ropes of their sleds, frozen themselves after a ride of almost endless glee.

"David, I hate to say it but I think we're stuck. Goddammit, this happens once a year. *Always* at the wrong time." The tires whirred on but failed to penetrate the ice. His father threw the car into reverse, then into drive, and the back end slid around slightly. "That's all we need. The car'll be here until March."

"Do you want me to drive?" David asked.

"Not unless you think you could handle it any better," his father said, looking at David.

"It's worth a try, don't you think? I mean, here we are."

"No," his father said. He put a hand to his chin. "I think we'll get out and walk. You don't have that much stuff. Then when I go to the station I can just back it down. Tonight I'll get a running start."

"All right."

"Some day, isn't it, David? Isn't it?"

And David got out of the car.

His father insisted on carrying the duffel bag up to the house but had considerable difficulty even lifting it onto his shoulder. David carried only his kit bag. He was wearing his winter uniform and an overcoat; fortunately in California he had had the foresight to remove them from the duffel bag. Before actually abandoning the car he had time to inspect carefully the right rear tire, which was causing all the trouble. He thought that his father, with luck, might be able to back the car down again, but it would take much more than a running start to get back up the hill in the evening.

"You know, we're sort of trapped up here. Did you ever think of that?" David asked.

"All the time," his father said. He looked ridiculous, like some olive-drab Santa Claus, half stooped over with the mammoth bulging duffel bag on his shoulder. "Couldn't you have just *shipped* these books home?" He stopped, and said quietly, "I am going to have a heart attack."

David took the duffel bag from him. They had only walked about ten yards from the car, but his father had to admit that the hill was a little too steep, the terrain a little too uncertain.

It seemed to David that something more than a physical burden had been removed from his shoulders. "I'll carry the small bag," he said. "I'm getting old. Ancient of days who sitteth throned in glory. *God,* it's a nice day, don't you think? Aren't you glad to be home?"

"Yes," David said. "Very glad." But he didn't quite know how he felt. He had been yanked around in time so much these past days.

"I wish I didn't have to go to work."

"Why don't you take the day off?"

"I wish I could. We might take a walk or something."

"I'd like that." *It would certainly be a first,* David thought.

His father looked at David. He said gently, "You must have lost at least thirty pounds."

They stopped and David lighted a cigarette. His father let the kit bag fall and put his hands in his pockets. After a minute he asked, "Did you write your sister Emily a lot?"

"Once a week," David replied.

"Then she knows pretty much what it was all about, I suppose."

"Pretty much. I didn't want to bother you," David said.

"I see. Did you write anybody else? Besides us, I mean."

He hesitated. "I heard from Elise a couple of times."

"Oh, yes," his father said quietly. "Elise."

David's former girlfriend was a subject that made his father a little uncomfortable.

"And Stewart, of course. My roommate at Harvard."

His father smiled and dropped Elise. "Well, I find that one must keep friendships in constant repair."

David felt an extraordinary sense of bewilderment and

dislocation when he looked up at the house. Jake, the family gardener, shuffled across the driveway, snow boots unlaced, hand outthrust to David, snow shovel in the other hand, with a gap-toothed smile. David felt like sitting down in the snow and saying Wait a minute, hold everything. Let me get my bearings. Don't spring everything on me at once.

David shook hands with Jake, who seemed actually moved to see him. Jake kept pumping his hand. David remembered how, the day before joining the Army, he had been sitting by the pool and Jake had come over with a live ground mole sitting blindly on a pitchfork. It was as if the ground mole was a little conversation-starter, an icebreaker, so that Jake could pass on his own Army experiences from World War II. And the ground mole sat on the pitchfork between them as they talked that day; the next day his father drove David over to the Army.

His room had been repainted a light blue. It was small and its two windows faced the driveway. The room was ruled by a large mahogany desk, the first piece of furniture David noticed when he walked in. His father had put the kit bag on a bureau by the door. David left the duffel bag upright, took off his overcoat and hung it in the closet. He went back to the duffel bag, rummaged inside for a moment, removed his toilet kit and went into the bathroom. He came out after he'd finished washing, did the best he could to straighten his uniform, decided not to take off his wet shoes and socks. He was exhausted; he had not slept in a day and a half.

There was now the matter of his mother. He took a deep breath before heading down to her room. You never knew what the situation was. As a child he would sometimes hold his breath until he got well into her room; the little boy. Sometimes his natural watchfulness became so avid that he forgot he was holding his breath until the absence of oxygen started him gasping.

If his mother was smoking Kents with the Micronite filter, or L&M's, that meant she was having a good day; though L&M's often indicated a pivotal change, a kind of balancing, a suspension bridge between moods.

But if she was smoking Salems or anything mentholated, then she was not having a good day, and David had to decide how not-good it was going to be. He knew this quite early in the morning and informed his sister Emily, or vice versa: Kent, L&M's or Salems. Sometimes he smelled tobacco when none was around.

His mother had two temperaments during her Salem days: awful, terrible. Each of these might or might not be preceded by a "simply," and "simply" meant that her children were intrusions, like hallucinatory multipedes.

After a year away, David knew something was wrong when he took a deep breath and didn't smell tobacco. He'd been hoping for a Kent kind of day, because he had just had the longest conversation of his life with his father, right out there on the driveway. A couple of inconsequential minutes, meditations upon a stuck car, but David really believed he was on a roll. One conversation might lead to another.

He felt fatigued yet alert, all jittery, tasting the air outside his mother's room, normally saturated but now devoid of any mood-clarifying smell. His eyes darted this way and that in the narrow corridor, just in the seconds before reaching the door. He thought of Emily and hoped they wouldn't have to think up new mood signals if their mother had quit smoking.

It was not without its humor, he recognized that; cigarettes and hierarchies of moods. Yet the sheer quickness of childhood assessments, still being made at the age of twenty-one, was pathetic. What truly amazed him was the face he put on for the occasion. With the absence of smoke signals to give her away—something different lurking in that bedroom—he felt himself lighting up; a foreign grin, a strut through the door. If she had been on the skids when he left, there was no telling what she was like now.

The door was half open and he knocked gently, and she said, "David, is that you?"

"Yes, Mom," he said. "It's me."

"It's been a year." She sat under blankets on one side of the double bed. "A whole year."

He was genuinely shocked by her appearance. He leaned over and kissed her, resting one hand lightly on her back, between the pillows, against the fabric of her nightgown. "You haven't changed," he said, still smiling, making an effort to compose himself.

"They treat me like an invalid."

His cheek came away moist. He heard the sound of a shower coming from his father's dressing room, then raised his head and looked at her, pleasure fully coordinated on his face, not a trace of surprise. His outward calmness sometimes got mistaken for a lack of feeling. In fact, he was often just trying to assess the amount of damage that the sight of something would do.

He wanted to say to his mother, *What in the name of God*

has happened to you? What is wrong? She sat like a shadow in the bed, gray skin and prominence of bones. The cleanliness of the smoke-free environment made him think of a surgical procedure; the patient lifted gently and examined. And the inevitability of deathbeds.

He would speak to his mother, but already in David's mind their conversation had been wrapped up and he was gone; he was outdoors in the previous winter sharpness of morning, where he could catch his breath. Even as they exchanged first words, his mother had become a part of the history of the day.

His mother said, "I wish you didn't have to see me like this."

"You look fine," David said firmly. "Really."

"I don't, darling. This terrible cold's lingered almost the whole winter. I can't seem to shake it. One day I'll feel fine and say to myself, Today we make an effort, but next day I'll feel just awful."

"It's the cold-and-flu season," David said reassuringly, amazed by his smoothness. His words emanated from a television commercial of the mind, but it was necessary for him to say that—to share with his mother that winter world out there of people stuffed up.

Once his mother grasped that no alterations had been made in their complicity—despite the ravages of a year—she felt free to luxuriate in her varied symptoms, all framed by a lingering bad cold. Chills, headaches, diarrhea, dizzy spells and weaknesses; long, white, blank days in bed. His mother put a hand to her head to indicate how splitting it had all been.

In the past these "colds" became so severe that his mother had to be put in storage—as David thought of it—for long periods of time, like a fur. Rural storage up at a special place in Connecticut; occasionally urban storage at a building in Manhattan that looked from the outside like the best private club.

His mother always returned from storage absolutely as a new woman, as if she had been given injections of vitality. Ceaseless hope is the tragedy of children; David always started again with this new woman. She made him giddy, gave him energy.

Inevitably, the cigarettes changed, the slide began, the girlish laughter got an edge. It was just a matter of time before it became necessary to put her back in storage for a while and get the poisons out of her system.

She was consistent about her relapses. That was just as well from David's point of view, because there was always an undercurrent of panic to his own delight; waiting. It was exhausting living through a month or so of cresting triumphs, like being on a winning streak you know can't possibly continue.

The best people were on her case, in Connecticut and Manhattan and all the hospitals in between, but David could have told them—judging from extensive clinical experience as her son—that she was incurable.

He never understood whether it was genetic or psychological or a cocktail of the two, but she returned to alcohol as one might return to thoughts of a lover who has left inexplicably. And alcohol loved her; the feeling was entirely mutual. You could see how it physically enlarged and gave her a substance that she lacked, how it swelled her in her chair and made her acceptable to herself.

His mother patted her hair with a quick, almost guarded movement. She said happily, "I ordered everything you like for supper. But you're so thin, darling. Didn't they feed you at all?"

"I never had much of an appetite." David took a step away from the bed. "Nobody ate very much."

"There's so much news," she said. "Everybody's called to ask about you. I have all the messages. Stewart, your old roommate, called three times last week. He wants you to go into New York and have dinner with him."

"I see," David said. "I'll give him a call." But Stewart seemed light-years away, a friend in some other life.

"Who is this girl Jane, what's-her-name?" his mother asked. "I'm dying to know."

"She called?" he asked, startled.

"Just once. The new maid spoke to her. She wanted to know when you were getting home."

David turned away. "She's just a friend."

His mother's voice sounded vague and a little baffled, as if connections weren't being made that should be made. "Jane. Jane. I don't think I know any Jane, do I?"

"No," David said quietly. "Actually, I've never met her either. She's the wife of a friend of mine in the Army." He couldn't bring himself to say "was."

"Then *she's* not the friend," his mother said. She would go along for a while without lucidity, then something would click.

"Well, no," David said hesitantly. "That's right. I've never met her."

His mother sounded relieved. "I didn't *think* Jane was familiar." She brightened considerably. "Now, Elise Morneau, I recognized her voice. It didn't seem, though, that I'd heard from her for a long time. Of course, why would she call, with you away?" She paused. "How stupid of me."

"Oh, sure. Elise," David said, hoping they would glide beyond all this. It bothered him a little that he was counting on his mother's fogginess. This was a very painful subject, Elise.

"Well, tell me everything," his mother said, and meant it. "Did you write each other often? I don't mean to pry. You two. Good Lord, I just couldn't believe it had been a whole year since I'd seen both of you."

They came as a boxed set, he and Elise. You got two for the price of one; his father had once said that about them. They even looked alike when in real physiology there was no resemblance. He was blond and she was dark; he was tall, she was short—or "petite," as his mother liked to say, with some acid—and on it went; he looked athletic, she looked frail. He was American; she was French. Probably there had been some gradual and even slightly comic mix-up in their gestures ever since childhood that caused people to see a resemblance when none existed. He had often wondered about that.

All of a sudden it made him sad, thinking about Elise, having her as close as a telephone call. He hadn't expected any mention of her, and here she was in the conversation.

Gently, sliding away from the subject, the brazen smile, his hands in the pockets of his uniform, feeling warm instead of cozy, beads of perspiration high on his forehead. "It's hard for me to believe, too," he told his mother. "It doesn't seem like a year. Time went by so fast."

Which wasn't true: the last year had been an endless catastrophe.

"Well, how is she?" his mother asked sharply, waiting on an answer, the hand going around her back to prop up a pillow. "Elise, I mean."

"We broke up," David said. "Before I left."

"Oh." There was a sharp shift of gears and the instantaneous spread of ill-concealed relief across her face. "I didn't know."

"I meant to tell you, and then I just thought, Why bother? I didn't much want to talk about it, anyway." Part of the reason he didn't tell her was that he did not want to see that look of relief.

"Of course not, darling," his mother soothed. She began to fidget with her hands, and finally whatever it was in there simply became irrepressible and activated her entire body with more energy than David believed she was capable of; just bubbled up and shook her, cut through the fogbanks of self-absorption. "You know, I never entirely approved of you two. Still, it just kills me."

And then she flung herself upon the words, striking them with her voice ferociously. "Well, I'm not going to offer advice and I'm not going to pry, but you've been inseparable since the first grade. David and Elise, Elise and David. That's all I've ever heard. You were far closer to Elise than you ever were to Emily, and Emily's your *sister,* for God's sake. Now,

I'm not going to pry, but obviously it's for the better. And now I've said my piece and I'll shut up.'' But she didn't, couldn't; she was actually quivering. ''As you know, I don't like everyone.''

David nodded seriously.

''And, as you know, I think that Elise's stepfather is one of the biggest loudmouths I've ever met in my life.''

''Yes,'' David said quietly. ''We have spoken about him before on several occasions.'' Understating her, mocking her ever so gently.

''At parties he . . . *slobbers*. There is no other word for it. He just plain slobbers—all over you—and yells at the top of his lungs right into your ear. I detest false heartiness, anyway, as you know.''

''Yes,'' David said gravely. ''As do I.''

''Even your father can't stand Corky Talbot, and that's saying something . . . Now, the *mother* is another story. The verdict is not in on Chantal Talbot. Of course, she *looks* as if she stepped right out of *Vogue,* and that's all very well. But I've always found her just a bit . . . distant.'' His mother nodded to herself sagely. ''Never less than polite; she has done many kind things for me during my illnesses. One is grateful for that when one is in poor health.''

His mother came upon her revelation then as she always did, quite by accident. And the very thought seemed to make her happy, seemed to wrap up the whole situation from which Elise Morneau had sprung. The girlfriend. ''Do you know what it's a case of?'' she asked. ''Chantal and Corky Talbot?'' Nodding vigorously to herself.

"Beauty and the Beast," David said distractedly. He regretted stepping on her best line, but it wasn't the first time.

"Exactly!" his mother exclaimed. "Beauty and the Beast. My God. And then you have poor Elise, literally *dropped* into that situation. You know, I always felt sorry for her, ever since she arrived from France. She was such a pathetic little thing. You would have thought she was a refugee, some homeless waif—not a little girl taking up a new life in that great barn of a house Corky's got in Oyster Bay. Well, it was just the saddest thing to see. One day with Corky must be a century. Lord, all that hot breath, and the sheer noise he kicks up."

Corky isn't so bad, David thought. But his mother had really sunk her teeth into Corky and Chantal and Elise. The delicious bloat of gossip had suddenly enlarged her. Now there was substance under the blankets. David suspected that for a long time she had been dying to talk to someone. "Did you ever meet Elise's real father, by the way?" his mother asked.

David shook his head. "No, I never did." There seemed to be no way of getting off this topic—snapshots of the girl were now in his mind, his life and her life—until his mother had run her course. He was almost willing to talk about war to get off this particular topic; he was almost nostalgic for the present.

"A real smoothie," his mother declared, and the slang pinned Elise's father to the wall. Her eyes became slits of character recognition: she had seen this type before; they cropped up usually during wartime when the husbands were away. "He was over here once on business, years and years ago. Who knows *what* business? A suave little hand-kisser with slicked-back hair and a funny suit, terribly French. They say he was a duke or a count or a prince, but"—and here his mother made aileron motions with her hand to indicate total dubiousness—"who's checking? I thought he was a hustler, pure and simple. He had this wretched charm . . . anyway, the word on him was commodities, but God knows it could have been anything."

His mother gave a weighty sigh; the suppurating human condition spread out before her. "Poor Elise. She grew up with a wild boor for a stepfather and a mother who ought to be back in France where she belongs, modeling clothes for Christian Dior. Not that I don't like Chantal. She brought me Lindt chocolates once and sat at the foot of this bed and we laughed like sailors. It's more a question of *belonging,* I think."

It wasn't apropos of anything, but David remembered a platoon sergeant during basic training at Fort Dix who hadn't liked his prep-school accent and had made him crawl under the barracks and bark like a dog. Not just one dog, but loud imitations of different breeds; poodle, terrier, St. Bernard and a memorable golden retriever.

"Yes," his mother concluded, with a sigh. "Beauty and the Beast. One simply can't conceive of them together, but of course they *are* together, aren't they? Chantal and Corky."

In moments he would have to step in and abruptly change, or catapult, the subject. And to think she had been so prostrate and gray when he had come into the bedroom. Her very skin might have been sheets.

"What *happened?*" his mother asked. "Between you and Elise. I don't mean to pry. You know that."

David shrugged. "She didn't want me to go in the Army, and things deteriorated from there."

His mother nodded snappily, as if this was confirmation of detective work she had been doing on her own. "I simply refuse to discuss the Army," she said then, with resigned nobility. Her whole being sagged into the bed; her head seemed to become unpropped from among the pillows and looked wayward. "I refuse to discuss it."

"Good," David said, relieved. "Let's not."

It was irresistible. "Your father and I were shocked. Of course, your father would never say anything, but *I* can tell you everything now that you're home safe and sound and my prayers have been answered. I owe it to myself to tell you. Neither of us could believe it. You had this brilliant future— Groton, Harvard. You had the brains, you had the looks, good heavens, the world was your oyster. And you threw it all away. It was the only thing you've ever done in your life that was utterly inexplicable. You were always the steady one. Now, if it had been your sister Emily . . . You know, I wouldn't be the least surprised if Emily popped into this room one morning and said, 'Mummy, I've decided to join the WACs,' or, 'Mummy, I'm pregnant but I don't know who the father is.' She is completely uncontrollable. There's a screw loose somewhere in that girl, mark my words. But *you*—you were always so *manageable.* You chugged right along as if you were on a little railroad track. I suppose those are the ones who commit the ax murders . . ."

His mother sometimes forgot to put a governor on her streams-of-consciousness.

"Well really," she said abruptly, conclusively, and not a

little huffily. "I couldn't have been more surprised if you'd joined the circus."

It had probably been half a year since something was funny. But David saw brightly dressed midgets climbing out of a tiny car, and that was all it took. He was off then, and he put out his hand toward his mother as if to ward off further humor. She looked bright and girlish and a little flustered for a moment.

"Sorry," David gasped, his eyes brimming, his body doubled with deep bends of laughter. He really ought to get some sleep; he'd been through a lot of time zones.

The circus.

"Well," his mother said tentatively, "I'm glad you're home. All of that is in the past."

He exhaled with the wheeze of an old person, put out his hand again apologetically. He saw himself in a black suit at the head of a long conference table, conducting a serious, bankerly meeting, but then these midgets leaped out of their little car again and ran around a sawdust ring under bright lights, and he felt eruptions of laughter from his side of the bedroom, coming to him from a distance. These midgets just kept running out.

At last he was calm again, and said, "Oh," still feeling delicately balanced, as if he had just had a narrow escape from something.

His mother looked at him with pity and bafflement. It was a nice reversal, since that was exactly how David had looked at her when he had first entered the bedroom. Her sandy face said, *What is going on?* Whatever happened to the little boy chugging purposefully along on his own private railroad track?

His mother summoned dignity, as a teacher would who was trying to restore order in an unruly classroom. "Now that you're home safe and sound—thank God for that . . . I know it's awfully early, but could you give your poor mother a clue, darling, about the future? Just to put my fevered mind at rest."

"I don't know, really. I'll take a month or so off, see some friends. I might get a job for a while, and then go back to school in the fall."

"You just get a nice rest," his mother said placidly, distantly. "Plenty of time to think about the future. Don't rush things." She seemed to become more alert then, as if something had synchronized. "That's always been Emily's problem. Fair game for any new experience, can't concentrate on anyone or anything for even a minute, hasn't a plan in the world. She's got youth on her side, but you can't go on *forever* burning the candle at both ends."

"Isn't she first in her class at school?" David asked, gently putting a lie to Emily's lack of concentration, her alleged candle-burning. "Yes, I think she mentioned that in one of her letters. Not that it means a hell of a lot to her."

"Everyone knows Emily is a genius," his mother sniffed, with some reflected pride in her voice. "But I really think she ought to have a hobby."

"Well, she's only seventeen. Give her a chance."

His mother looked haughty. "Sooner or later she's going to have to pay the piper."

David teetered, as mirth stoked his belly again. He put a

warning hand to his forehead. Something about the piper being paid, entranced children led out of town.

"After all, the purpose of life is to find a husband. Who's going to want to marry her in her condition?"

"Exactly what condition is that?" David asked.

"Wild," his mother said flatly. "First of all, she'd argue any upstanding young man to death. She fights over every little point, the most minute little thing. Men don't like that. No, you have to put them on a pedestal and pretty soon they toddle away happy as little lambs . . . Some of the men she's brought home this last year are not only *twice* her age but have no means of employment that I can discover. Of course I never pry. I just hope she doesn't wind up in some motorcycle gang at the age of eighteen, knocked up . . . When you think of all the nice boys from good families—the tea dances and cotillions we had when I was a girl . . . It breaks your heart because she has the looks, if she'd ever do something about her hair. She's not some ratty little thing off the streets. I wish she'd draw on my experience, just plunk herself down on the bed and *ask* sometime, but she never does. I seem to annoy her. Why is that?"

"I don't know," David said.

His mother patted her hair and sighed deeply for the fate of her wayward daughter. "She actually told me over Christmas that I *enjoyed* poor health. As if I *asked* to be sick. Emily can be so cutting, I'm afraid of her sometimes. I cringe. Afraid of her and afraid for her."

"How was she over Christmas?" David asked. "She hasn't written me in the last couple of months."

"Left in a huff," his mother said with a what-can-you-do

shrug. "Got in a terrible row with your father, stalked out without saying goodbye. Off to join her rowdy friends, doubtless. The company of her parents is much too tame for her. We expected a nice, peaceful Christmas—I haven't been at my best lately—and we got high drama. Honestly, Emily should consider an acting career. She has a flair; I don't know what else you'd call it."

"What did they argue about, do you remember?" David asked, alert now. "Dad and Emily, I mean."

"I have no idea, David. A tempest in a teapot. I heard her yelling like a fishwife, and you know how sensitive I am about noise. Of course, your father's used to dealing with her by now. God knows, I wouldn't have been surprised if he banished her from this house forever, especially after that business . . . We won't talk about that—one forgives and forgets and moves on—but it's a very black mark against your sister Emily. That was the first time it occurred to me I might have raised a juvenile delinquent."

"For God's sake, Mom," David said, annoyed. "That's really going too far."

"Is it now?" his mother asked. "A common *groom!* It is one thing to be oversexed, it's quite another to debase yourself with stableboys on your neighbor's estate."

"Okay," David said. "Enough."

"I rest my case," his mother declared.

What case? David wondered.

"Not to mention the horses," his mother continued. "To this day I have dreams about those poor, beautiful, dumb animals. I'd rather see a man run over than a horse. Do you know how much those horses were worth?"

"A lot," David said quietly.

"In excess of one million dollars. Thoroughbred racing horses, *destroyed* because some oversexed teenager wants excitement on her spring vacation. One million dollars. I don't think for a moment that Emily set out deliberately to bring disgrace upon her family, but the end result was the same."

"I don't think she brought disgrace upon this family," David said. "It was an accident and everybody knows it was an accident. I mean, everybody makes mistakes. It's always possible to misjudge people. I don't know why we're getting so down on Emily. Why don't we change the subject?"

"The police hunted him down and arrested him in Binghamton, New York. He didn't have a dime to his name and *reeked* of turpentine. How's *that* for misjudging character? This family would have had to endure the horror of a trial in which Emily would have had to testify about her relationship with that scum. Fortunately, the young man did the decent thing and hanged himself in his cell."

David was losing it. He wanted to back up the film and start all over again at the moment when he had first got home. He would have done everything differently. He would have kissed his mother, had a few minutes' talk, been out the door again—polite, neat, short. Somewhere he had gone wrong.

"Believe it or not, we're *still* on speaking terms with the Jepsons. Can you believe it—Roger Jepson put his arm around your father and said, 'The old guard has to stick together.' A-men to that. Looking right out at the same Long Island Expressway that sliced his property in *half*."

His mother seemed meditative for a moment, and David

guessed she was winding down now. "I suppose she's"—he assumed his mother meant Emily, though now he sensed a drifting of her mind—the loosening of its moorings—as her head settled back into the pillows and the ceiling began to occupy her eyes—"been spoiled rotten. Everything's always been laid out for her on a silver platter. She must think she can just stamp her pretty little foot like some fairy-tale princess or wave a magic wand and everything will be done for her. But life has its harsh side, I've found. Don't you agree?"

David was surprised his mother remembered he was in the room. He nodded. "Yes, it certainly does."

His mother sighed and her head sank more deeply and tiredly into the pillows. "Here I've been rattling on. It's because I've been so lonely. This terrible cold lingers and lingers and saps my energy. But now I want to hear all about *you*. Tell me about Baghdad."

"Baghdad?" David asked gently. The thief of Baghdad? Baghdad on the Hudson?

His mother put a hand to her forehead. "I mean Bangkok."

"Actually, I never quite made it to Thailand," David said, maintaining that gentle tone.

"Where *is* my head at?" his mother asked, confused. "Sometimes I wonder."

"I did get to Hong Kong, though. That was beautiful. Unfortunately, we had to get there by ship. It reminded me of the troop transport we took to Vietnam. I wrote you about working in the butcher shop."

"Yes, I remember something . . ."

"And I spent a week in Tokyo. I had a choice between Bangkok and Tokyo, but I chose Japan because my friend was interested in a Japanese painter, Hiroshige, and he also wanted to take the bullet train and look at Mount Fuji. That was good enough for me.''

''They have lovely silks in Bangkok.''

''They do indeed,'' David said and blew out a long breath. ''I never made Angkor Wat either. My friend was very interested in seeing all these places. He had a way of making the best of a bad situation. If it hadn't been for him I probably wouldn't have gone to either Hong Kong or Japan. I guess it's a little bit like cabin fever: you know you ought to get out, but you think, What's the point? My friend had a quickness. Probably he just wanted to be anywhere except where he was.''

He had the sudden consciousness of a vast, vacant verbal space occupied only by himself. It was part of the loneliness he always felt in this house of self-absorption. Loneliness followed by restlessness and the need to be on his way.

He got up and paced around the bedroom. He didn't really want to get into Baghdad now, though he had been looking forward to talking with *someone* about it for a long time. For the life of him—as he paced around, the tiniest bit caged—he couldn't remember where Baghdad was. Morocco? Egypt?

It was quite remarkable, he noticed, how his mother filled up with herself all over again, how the color of her own words came into her cheeks. David felt grateful that they were now off the subject of his sister Emily, and into benign areas: a new servant, a vacation in Hobe Sound, Fisher's Island, the Mill Reef Club, people seen. Nothing special, nothing really interesting, but David couldn't help but notice the long blank stretches in his mother's life when she was evidently out of commission.

He paced around and looked at the photographs of his mother scattered on walls and tables around the bedroom. Most of them had been taken at a time when her victories had been as real as trophies. A young woman of grace and beauty stared back at him. She strode purposefully along a fairway with her long legs; she held a golf club and smiled for the camera; she was captured on the follow-through of a beautiful swing. She stood at the center of a group shot, holding a silver cup nearly her size.

Once upon a time her touch had been golden, but David knew of this other woman only through photographs. He knew in person only a woman whose legs and reflexes were long gone and who had taken up backgammon, bridge— games sometimes cutthroat, mostly boozy. The photographs showed better times, when the fairways had been spacious and she had been amateur golf champion of three states. All the trophies were in the attic now, turning black.

He had always thought of his mother as being amazingly clumsy, frequently bruised from bumps and slides and slips and knockings-into. Sometimes she moved with a phony grace—there was no other way to describe it—and to David she looked like a woman who was seconds away from falling into an empty swimming pool. She had a precarious kind of blitheness.

Emily had traces of the woman his mother must have been. She embodied a kind of history of his mother and offered a link with some graceful mythical past before he was born. What baffled him about both his mother and his sister was that here they were, blessed with immense physical gifts—hand-eye coordination, super eyesight and tall lean bodies—natural athletes, both of them—and each of them squandered their talents, each in a different way—really, in what he regarded as an almost criminal way. His mother took to drinking, but at least she had had her trophy moments. Emily in his mind was inexcusable, because she picked up and dropped all the sports you could think of; so all you were left with was this momentary dazzlement: the racquet or club or stick, the flash, the shrug, and that was that. Time to move on.

When his mother's legs went, she took up bridge, and that was where David and Emily came in, much too late for what they thought of as the "good years."

David didn't mind bridge; it kept his mother occupied for afternoons. He could keep tabs on her because frequently the games were held at their house. He didn't like it when she got in the car to go off to someone else's house, especially if it was a new player. His mother was a bad driver, but it helped when David could mentally do aerial reconnaissance of her planned route, telepathically noting the dangers for her: curves and big trees. But with a new route for a new player he was frantic with imaginary maps. Where the hell was Wolver Hollow Road? Chicken Valley Road? Where was Exit 51S on the Long Island Expressway? Not that telepathy helped much, though his mother never had the big accident that David feared. Instead, she was an insurance adjuster's wet dream: fender-benders, dents, broken headlights, long scratches and weird rippling crumples; the continual minor scarring of her vehicle, as if it had been to battle.

His mother was a good bridge player, but when her brain

got marinated either she stopped playing or nobody wanted to play with her anymore. There were the four women in a smoke-filled room where too much vodka flowed surreptitiously and gossip flew. At the end of the afternoon the women staggered to their cars. Except for the hazardous driving, David thought bridge was a pretty harmless activity for older women whose husbands were spending the same afternoon at their clubs in the city. Life was hardly taxing, but everyone made a big thing out of pretending they lived like other people; it made them democratic to themselves, which is the key to American upper-class life. Cars, timetables, ball games, any kind of slang on the airwaves—and you would not believe the comparison shopping. David had heard people over glasses of champagne at Thanksgiving rave about the cheapest Butterball; having driven all over Long Island to find it, having dug through every frozen-food case.

Bridge filled his mother's afternoons; otherwise she would have started drinking before lunch. She seemed to pride herself on showing up for games with a clear head. Then the women got into the vodka or the Dubonnets as the afternoon lengthened. Sometimes, if the game was held at his house, David would pop into the living room, timing his unobtrusive arrival to coincide with the moment when the gossip reached maximum juiciness. Most of the women were so ripped by then that self-censorship was meant for another life.

Emily's reaction to the bridge games was inexplicable. It was just another example of how she always went too far. She invented fierce nicknames for the players. One he remembered: Spider Belly. When the women rose in the afternoon and made their way to the bar or to the little girls' room, their arms were raised as if dangling from puppet strings, and they made mincing dance steps, like a weird cha-cha-cha.

"Did you see?" Emily would whisper to him. "Every time Spider Belly tosses back that black, black bourbon, I swear her arms sprout hair . . . Look, look . . . Listen to that laugh. Doesn't it sound like she owns the biggest whorehouse in town?" The two whispering, hatching conspirators among all those adults.

Listening now to his mother in the bedroom, he missed Emily. He was back on Long Island, back to the world of the house. Everything had sunk in at last.

You never knew what the hell Emily would do next— sweep out of the house, make some withering comment, ventilate enthusiasms, stand on her head. She was perpetually engaged in some titanic struggle to declare herself. It was as though if she stopped the struggle even for a moment, silence and stillness and death awaited her.

David would have been glad for a little of Emily on this morning. Beyond the bedroom nothing existed except more silence: a houseful and the acres beyond. He was home, and he squinted against the wintry light.

He kind of wandered around for a few last minutes, his mother telling him of the escapades of the latest maid, who held parties on the terrace when the family was away. But you could forgive anyone anything as long as they *showed up*.

The shades had been drawn on two of the four windows. The fireplace crackled, a full log bin on either side. As he paced, his eye finally caught the large mirror before her dressing table and he stopped to look at the snapshots wedged between the frame and the glass. One picture showed the family standing on the lawn, Emily holding a dog David didn't remember, everyone looking faintly hostile and weary. The mirror also held engraved invitations, each with a thinly penned regret at the top corner.

His mother rested against the pillows with her hands in her lap. She looked thoroughly exhausted now, very sickly, with no trace of the colored emotions—jealousy, bitterness, depression, anger, utter bafflement—that had fired her cheeks just minutes before.

David settled into a chair at the far end of the room. He kept his eyes on a point a little above her.

In a few minutes his father came out of his dressing room and into the bedroom. He wore a dark three-piece suit and looked dignified standing at the far end of the room.

"Well, I'm off," he said vaguely. Then for some reason he went over and shook hands with David. There was nothing awkward about it; just a quick move around the bed. He gripped his son's hand for an extra second and looked at him carefully. David was still seated but would have risen if his father hadn't been so close.

"I trust I shall see you for dinner," his father said.

David really envied his father—the hum and routine of his business life. The family bank in New York, the hush of its corridors, the beginnings and retirements, the history of it stretching back to the early nineteenth century.

Everything was continuity. David thought there was a lot to be said for that; continuity. It must be immensely satisfying to know what the day will bring.

He liked having lunch with his father in the private dining

room at the bank. The way everything moved along, like being inside a fine piece of machinery. It was almost as if the bank were in the business not of making money but of making things run smoothly. He had felt so secure at the bank—amid the paneling, with the centuries of partners looking down benignly from the walls.

Smoothness and continuity, but also a bottom line. You added up the figures, and they didn't lie.

"I'll walk you to the car, if you don't mind," David said.

"I know, you're just going to make some comment about my driving," his father said with a smile.

"Come on," David told him, on his feet. "You'll miss your train."

In mock sorrow his father put his hand on David's shoulder. Then, because he really was in a hurry, he walked over and kissed David's mother perfunctorily, told her when he would be home and left the room. These two strangers were his parents and there was not a second's intersection of feeling between them.

When David met him in the front hall his father carried a brown briefcase and had put on a different, newer overcoat.

David stood on the last stairstep. He put his hands in his pockets and leaned against the banister. "I'm really worried. She looks terrible, even worse than when I left, if that's possible."

His father held tight to the briefcase. "Yes," he said. "She has been unwell."

"That's the understatement of the year."

His father kept his free hand at his side and his back slightly arched, as if David were at a great height. "Yes, well, I'll see you tonight then."

"Okay," David said.

"Seven or so. I hope you'll stay here for a while, before you make any permanent plans and so on."

"Yes, I'd like to."

"Now if I can get the bloody car down the hill."

"I'll come out and help if you want."

"No," his father said. "In the privacy of my dressing room I thought up an almost foolproof plan. A little something I picked up from the Italian racing drivers."

"I wondered," David said. "Is Mom going away again?"

"No," his father replied. "That isn't in the game plan at the moment."

The game plan. Ultimately, there was no way of reaching him, but David felt badly that he had put it quite that way—going away again—because it sounded as though his mother was being put to sleep.

David watched from the door as his father moved down the driveway, swinging his briefcase back and forth. Then suddenly his father slipped, the briefcase flew out of his hands, and he fell into the snow.

David wanted to call to him, but kept silent as his father slowly picked himself up, brushed the snow carefully from his overcoat, then went over and picked up the briefcase. He walked down the driveway, and his son watched him until he had rounded the curve.

David had planned things, but nothing seemed to jell. He took long walks in the country, through the last sections of fields and woods left on the North Shore of Long Island. He would put on his boots, see his mother and then start off through the winter day in no particular direction—in the woods, along the bridle paths, into snow-covered fields.

There would be no precise beginning or end to it, just one moment he would be running in the woods, along the narrow bridle paths soft in their first thaw. His steps would upset listening rhythms: a black-eyed cardinal would take off in a burst of red; a rabbit would flee onto the path and launch a zigzag run along its corridor; a dove like hurled snow would shoot from the trees.

He would run for perhaps a mile, until his breath came in cold satisfying gasps. He would run upon horse jumps across the trail—of logs or thick wooden rails—and take them, his feet splashing into hoof-cut snow on the other side. He would slow down when through the trees he could see the steadying white of a field.

He was out walking one morning and he recognized the horse and the girl from a distance, and seeing her approach him he felt something like a dizzy spell, but it was the rush of jealousy.

The unscathed quality of Elise and her new boyfriend, who was impeccable—as if his riding clothes had been laid out for him, along with all the other clothes he needed to face the day. So cool, both of them, and David looked unusually scruffy and muddy, as if he'd been stomping in puddles with his combat boots.

So, they approached unavoidably along a narrow path that ran beside hedges concealing an estate. David was even annoyed by the boyfriend's riding helmet, which sat a little too firmly on his head. This was the way a riding helmet sat. And he didn't like the idea of having to talk *up* to the two of them. He also didn't like the idea that he had made a grievous error by wasting two years—just bloody wasting them, as though they had been ripped out of his life—and this guy, you could tell, had been living pretty high on the hog during those same years; had probably traveled to Europe and dined in fine restaurants, been a weekend guest.

David went from zero to sixty in about three seconds. He became a social accident waiting to happen. It had never occurred to him that things might be going well for her. There was certainly a lot of animation in the old saddle; a lot of Gallic gesturing; and a conversation in which he was not a participant. He felt betrayed by her.

Elise took a long time to recognize him, even though he waved. He had lost weight, of course; he needed a shave, a haircut; he wore his field jacket, which she had never seen before. These were points in Elise's favor. Still, you'd think that, having known each other for sixteen years—more than a decade and a half of continuous friendship—permanent vibrations would have been established between them.

Instead, she turned away from her boyfriend a couple of times, in the fullness of their animation, and seemed to *squint* toward the walking figure, unsure whether to return the wave.

He wanted to disappear; he should have turned around and gone home. But his spontaneous wave and the quick gladness in it, really almost innocent, had exposed him. He was now part of the threesome. He could no longer just drift into the landscape and keep going.

When the fun-loving couple was no more than twenty yards away, David began to raise questions about their patriotism. He knew that was pretty low even by the standards of this cold, sunken morning, but he couldn't help himself. *These* were the people he had fought for, with their horseback lives and high teas.

This chance encounter startled him, made him realize he missed everything about Elise. Later he would gather her gestures and replay them: the big eyes widening, the sound of his name, which stretched French-like into something like Dahveed. Had she spoken it above a whisper, the word would have made her sound exactly like her mother, Chantal, whose French accent had grown more pronounced through the rich years in America.

Elise no longer had a French accent, though once upon a time, dropped into Long Island from the sky, she had been almost unintelligible. She prided herself on being as American as an immigrant's pride could make her, so obviously this throwback pronunciation just erupted in her throat.

Later, when David observed the disastrous scene from different angles, Elise bubbled right up before him, practically standing in her stirrups, and he could see for himself how badly he had blown it.

With Elise's first recognition did not come a wave but a gesture in his direction, or a waver, delicately as if he were the intricate feature of some painting newly brought to light.

David took this in but focused his attention on the boyfriend's slurred British accent—upper-class, but with an odd, almost Cockney sound that would annoy anyone. It was on the borderline of actual gargling and presented piercingly in middialogue to the winter air.

Imagine what he sounds like indoors, David thought and made the slightest unbidden lip-twitch. Elise, beside the Englishman, appeared as cool as a cucumber.

Elise was a sweet person with a steely character encased in reticence. Bad manners were unbearable to her; unbearable was not too strong a word. A slight shift in tone got her full attention, and with rudeness she experienced tremendous pain.

"Just like fried eggs," her stepfather Corky Talbot used to call her eyes, taking some satisfaction in his served-up image. David never had to look beyond good old Corky to find the source of Elise's agony. Corky grabbed onto the great steer of life and twisted its neck all the way to the ground. Elise had once told David that being with Corky was like spending your childhood with a hideous stranger. Deeply ashamed of him, she had always yearned to be close to him. He was, for all his faults, her stepfather.

The three finally met on the lonesome trail. From high atop her chestnut hunter Elise said coolly, "David, how nice to see you again. It's been a long time."

The hunter nodded at him on the ground. Elise was so dainty, like a figurine atop the horse. She wore no helmet and looked a little white up there, wearing a tweed hacking coat, a charcoal-gray sweater over a thin white blouse; thick corduroy trousers; calf-high riding boots whose shiny toes pointed through the stirrups like black birds framed in silver. She wore no gloves, and her left hand looked almost welded to the reins, and her right hand kept flexing and unflexing, either to keep the circulation going or because the layer of coolness that she had assumed hadn't quite delivered the message of formality down to her extremities. So, something was itching like a trigger finger.

"Hi there, Elise." This is exactly what he said; the "hi" getting to him the most later on. "Great to see you." His smile felt pasted on and completely lopsided. The upper lip caught a little on his front teeth and made him look momentarily foxy.

His fake heartiness took Elise aback, and her brow knitted. "Oh, fine," she said quietly. "David Winant, let me introduce you to . . ."

And here is where everything went wrong, where David cleared the bases in one blow. "Rhys Pinklington Righter-Davies."

Or Pinkerton, or something, but anyway it took a beat or two longer to get out. Elise might even have flubbed the name in her scarcely concealed nervousness. But the fact was that it hung out there fatly, and David had his cut.

It was no accident that he brooded in baseball terminology whenever this scene presented itself later for his delectation and gave a tingle to his moroseness. Elise was an avid baseball fan. She felt it made her a member of the American Pageant, a fellow dreamer of the American dream. It had been the most civil sport she could find on short notice, having been dumped unceremoniously on our shores. Corky had a box at Yankee Stadium—practically on the field—and it was a way of having something in common with him. But Elise often went to the Polo Grounds on her own to catch the National League teams swinging through.

So, the Englishman's name hung out there ripely like the fattest pitch, and David felt a little popping in his head when he took his rip. The Englishman looked supercilious, which just added mustard and relish to the hot dog. He had a bloodless lankness about him, a bluish glider of a nose that he looked down.

But for months afterward David would shudder at his preconceptions and wonder if he was not a terribly nice guy once you got to know him.

"Jesus," David sputtered. "What kind of name is that?"

Elise tried to run David over with her horse. He saw the steel cast of her face, like paint peeled away; the tossed black hair; the green eyes turn to ice-emeralds in an instant. Politeness had always been the central mutuality between them. This thoughtless comment was the same as slugging her, really.

David leaped out of the way and the big animal, spurred, ran beyond him. He got just a glimpse then of Elise's teeth, her breath like a hiss, though she did not deign to violate the air with a single word to him. He would have felt deeply grateful for some kind of abuse.

"Well, it's *my* name, actually," the Englishman said sweetly, tipping his helmet, so polite that it was rather as if he had encountered another gentleman on the trail, not some ill-mannered fool.

David left the scene of the accident. He walked on up the trail, first with his hands in his blue jeans pockets; then he folded his arms across the chest of his field jacket, all hunched and weighty, mad with self-disgust.

And missing Elise; missing her even before she was ten

yards away with her impervious tweed back. He should have called her first thing when he got home; after all, she had called him. Oh, damn.

He continued walking through the woods, then came to a clearing and sat for a long time atop a post-and-rail fence that ran beside a long driveway. The word "jerk" kept occurring to him. He didn't want to go home just yet, not knowing how to fill up the remainder of the morning and afternoon. Without directly acknowledging it, he had been counting on Elise to help him with his life, his debilitating lack of purpose. When he finally got himself together—shortly, just a little farther down the road—she would have been the first person he'd have called.

He could forget that now.

An old man named Roger Jepson pulled up silently in his horse-drawn sleigh. "Hop in, David. I'll take you to the end of my driveway."

David realized that he had parked himself on the post-and-rail fence bordering the long driveway of the Jepson estate. The driveway was approximately three miles long and ran through white fields, ending in a Georgian brick mansion at the top of a hill, redly visible now across the fields like a dash of blood; where Mr. Jepson lived alone with his ailing wife.

Mr. Jepson's memory was nicely shot, so even though he hadn't seen David in two years, you could feel that with him time was an accordion. He recognized David instantly, the clean-cut boy behind the unshaven mess in the ratty field jacket. It was like the way color-blind people are used as spotters to see through camouflage. It was as if David and Mr. Jepson had seen each other just yesterday.

David hopped in and they glided down the center of the long driveway, with the slivers of maple-tree branches overhead. Mr. Jepson offered David a part of the yellow blanket draping his lap, and David accepted it gladly.

The horse was as black and shiny as you would think Black Beauty was in the book, and had a racehorse's delicacy of bone structure and a nice high step. The horse looked as if it were really heading somewhere instead of to the end of the driveway a mile away, where Mr. Jepson would turn the sleigh around and head home.

The whole effect—delicate racehorse, light sleigh, fragile Mr. Jepson, flickers of maple branch—made David feel almost airy also. This was as comfortable as he had been in a long time. He wanted to put his arms under the blanket and pull it over his shoulders so that just his face was exposed to the elements.

His father once told David that Roger Jepson was "the last of the great plunderers." He was probably eighty-five or ninety years old now, with a squat, immobile body and a blueberry-muffin face. David wondered if Mr. Jepson had ever told the public to be damned, kept U.S. senators in his hip pocket.

"He's a pleasant old codger," his father had once said. "I'm surprised he never got religion. Usually they get religion at the end. Atoning for a lifetime of pillage."

Mr. Jepson flicked the reins of his beautiful black horse. The runners of the sleigh made a lovely shushing sound, cautioning the passengers against excessive noise. "Welcome aboard, David," Mr. Jepson said heartily, as if they were going on the best voyage. "Haven't seen you in weeks."

David didn't feel he was humoring him when he said, "No, sir. I've been away." He wondered whether it was a good or bad thing to have time contracting and expanding like that, whimsically.

"You looked like Rodin's *The Thinker* back there," Mr. Jepson said. "I hope I didn't disturb you. Too nice for deep thoughts, good day for little thoughts."

"Actually, my thoughts weren't very deep," David said with a smile. It was conceivable he would fall asleep in this comfortable sleigh. He suddenly felt overwhelming tiredness, wondered if he could ask Mr. Jepson, when they got to the end of the driveway, to take him for another spin—or glide.

"It's good to get away," Mr. Jepson mused. His nose had a marvelous bluish glow. "The doctors made me give up drinking and cigars. I feel lousy."

"You look well, Mr. Jepson."

"Bullshit!" the old man yelled, and the black horse's ears shot up. "I look ninety."

"You look well for ninety." In fact, he didn't look a day over eighty.

"Dunno what that's supposed to mean," Mr. Jepson sulked. "I thought you two were an item."

"We were."

He meant Elise. You had to kind of drift along with him. He went from bellow to pussycat very rapidly, and it was up to you to find your bearings.

"She's got someone else," Mr. Jepson confided. "An English chap."

"How long has that been going on?" David asked with mild teeth-gritting.

"Years," Mr. Jepson said, which of course was impossible. "See them all over the place. All over the place. All over the bloody place. I wouldn't mind taking *her* on a little sleigh ride. What's her name again?"

"Elise Morneau."

"The father's a loudmouth, I hear."

"Stepfather," David said. "Yes."

"Why is everybody so coarse? You hire people and the first thing they want is a television."

"Then they start haggling about their half day off," David said, with just enough irony.

Mr. Jepson looked at David slyly. It was rare to see his eyes because they were set back very deeply and overlaid by bushy brows and thick lids. It was like seeing flits of blue between heavy clouds.

David wondered idly if perhaps Mr. Jepson had always been senile, even fifty years ago at the top of his game, and that had somehow worked for him down in the pits of finance.

"The doctors told me to give up drinking and cigars, so I got new doctors."

David nodded, but he wanted to get this off his chest. "Elise introduced me to this Englishman about fifteen minutes ago and he had a long name and I said, 'Jesus, what kind of name is that?' Just out of the blue. How could I say something like that?"

"The two of them look like goddamn models out of a magazine. I see them around here all the bloody time. And that limey just oozes politeness. That's what I like about you. You don't ooze."

"High praise."

"When Robert Moses was building the Long Island Expressway, I got him on the Ameche and I said, 'This is Roger Jepson, and I've got more lawyers than you've got fingers and toes.' You know what he did? Took *fifteen* of my acres."

"Anyway, I blew it. I guess that's why I was looking like a statue when you saw me."

"It wasn't like that in the old days," grumbled Mr. Jepson.

"What wasn't?" David asked, returning to the present.

"We had them move the Northern State Parkway, you know. Thirty years ago, when we first saw the plans."

"Moved where?"

"Oh, a few miles south. So it wouldn't interfere with our town."

"I didn't know that. You *moved* the Northern State Parkway?"

"A gang of us got together—some of the old families—and had a word with the governor and the appropriate state authorities."

"If you moved the Northern State Parkway, why couldn't you move the Long Island Expressway so it didn't go through your property?"

"Because we're all dead!" shouted Mr. Jepson. "And I'm not feeling too well myself." Then, in a more chastened voice, "Robert Moses told me, 'Roger, if it's the last thing I ever do, I'm going to put bulldozers in your paradise.' And he was as good as his word."

"He sure was," David said.

Mr. Jepson made another abrupt shift.

"You shouldn't blame Emily, you know," he said, making a

click sound to his striding black horse as they neared the end of the white sheet of driveway.

"Emily?" David asked, startled. "Oh, right. My sister."

Through the silence of their wonderful gliding, David could hear in the distance the steady hum of the Long Island Expressway, broken by the shiftings of diesel rigs.

"It wasn't her fault."

"I don't think anyone blames her, Mr. Jepson."

"Your father does," Mr. Jepson said flatly. "I know your father very well. I used to give Emily rides in this sleigh. The first thing she'd want to do was drive, then she'd take the reins, stand up and shout, 'C'mon, boy.' Took ten years off my life, but she'd get your motor running. I like that. Even if you fuck it up, *do* something . . . All the girls want it now. It's a new age. I didn't see a tit until I was twenty-eight. That was in 1903 . . . Where the hell was I?"

"About Emily," David said gently.

"They were *my* horses, David. If I'm not mad, then nobody should get mad. You don't like to see them ripped up like that. It was a weird and pathetic sight . . . Your father took it hard. He's a great gentleman and I'm his greatest fan, as you know, David. But he sets standards that are very hard to live up to. He must have a Puritan strain in there somewhere. Personally I've never had any standards, but live long enough and they think you're a philanthropist . . . After Emily's folly, I put my arm around your father and told him, 'The old guard has to stick together,' and he was moved. Yes, moved. It was just the right touch, but I don't think it got your sister Emily off the hook. How is she, by the way?"

"I haven't seen her for a while. She's down in Virginia at prep school."

"Tell her I miss our sleigh rides," Mr. Jepson said. "Maybe the horse doesn't, but I do."

"Thank you for the lift, Mr. Jepson."

"Good to see you, David. It's been weeks."

David got out of the sleigh and Mr. Jepson lifted a trembly hand in farewell. With little stops and starts he deftly turned the fragile sleigh around and set off again up the driveway. He looked sort of Christmasy as he faded into the distance, not without a last wave to David; more of an exhausted circular motion in the air, like a falling white bird.

David went out for dinner in New York with his Harvard roommate, Stewart, at a restaurant called Le Veau d'Or on East Sixtieth Street. He had been looking forward to talking with Stewart for a good long time. He needed to make some connection with his other self—the twenty-year-old Harvard student who had wanted to leave college and the soldier that student had become. There was a connection somewhere, if only he could make it.

What was impressive about Stewart was the total solidification of his life, the way everything had fallen into place. A gracious future stretched out before him, and he was ready to meet it. It was nice to be with him, after this long absence, because Stewart was his oldest friend; and, more important, Stewart had maintained a certain irony about his three-piece predicament; his Philadelphia lawyer of a father always breathing down his neck. Still, David felt a little envious of

Stewart, because his friend's life seemed to be in order, while his own wasn't.

"So when are you coming back to Cambridge?" Stewart asked.

"Probably in the fall," David said with a shrug. Cambridge was not necessarily in his plans, but it sounded good to him: Harvard, the little sliver of a future. It seemed to head off some line of questioning before it could quite get started. "I'm just taking it easy for now."

"Seen Elise?" Stewart asked, and David noticed his sudden nervous finger-tapping on the tablecloth.

"I have," David said. "She looked well."

"Did you meet the new friend?"

David nodded. "How did you know about him?"

"I heard. He's been around New York awhile. I guess it's a steady thing."

"He looked well, too. Everybody looks so goddamn *well*, Stewart."

"I called her. I don't know, six months, a year ago."

"And?"

"She let me down easy," Stewart said. "Then I heard she'd taken up with this Englishman. I think he's a lawyer, a barrister . . . What can you do . . . They ride together. Somebody told me all this."

"When I saw her last week, she tried to run me over with her horse. She was with him then."

Stewart seemed to brighten. "Really? Tried to run you over? Tell me about it."

"I said something that offended her."

"That's not like Mr. Polite."

"I don't know what came over me, Stewart," David said with a smile.

"I'm shocked. I gather it's completely over and done with between you two."

"Yes," David said dryly. "You could say that."

"Well, I guess I knew that. That's why I called her." Stewart was silent for a moment. "You made a splendid couple, by the way."

"Thank you, Stewart."

"It used to piss me off."

"I know. I never understood why."

"What did you have that I didn't have?" he asked with a certain moroseness.

"A bubbling personality?"

Stewart laughed. "A bubbling personality. That's good. But what *happened* between you two?"

David shrugged. "Ancient history. I'd rather hear more about your European tour, Stewart." He thought of Stewart's planned trip in capital letters: Stewart's European Tour.

"Why don't you come with me?" Stewart asked eagerly, resting his elbows on the table and leaning forward. Stewart was a golf nut. "We start in Scotland, move on to England, then the Continent. Obviously only the great golf courses in Scotland. St. Andrews, Troon. We'll hone our games as we go . . ."

David smiled, sat back, listened to Stewart describe his grand tour, which would consist partly of golf and partly of culture. However, if European culture didn't coexist with a golf course, it would have to go. A map of Europe turned green and smooth in David's mind as Stewart spoke. The world seemed for a few minutes not much more serious than a difficult pin placement.

Stewart said, "I'm glad you came back in one piece. Missed ya," which touched David, that "ya" especially touching.

But then anxiety assaulted David from all sides. The French of the restaurant—actually a lively bistro—suddenly hemmed him in with thoughts of Elise and thoughts of Vietnam. And then Stewart's simple question, such a simple goddamn question—"How was it over there?"—and the way Stewart leaned back in his chair, fingers touching the stem of his wineglass, to listen to David describe his grand tour of Vietnam.

The ferocity of his need to explain to the receptive Stewart was so powerful that the words—he never even got himself and Allen off the boat; they were still down in the ship's butcher shop—clogged his mouth and felt both enormous and weighty as if they had been specially cut from blocks. He was breathing through his mouth, as if he were running through all the marathon days of his grand tour.

Just for a second he thought he was having a heart attack, but he was too young, he decided—part of him musing, looking down upon himself.

The colors of the restaurant turned vivid white and black. The noise in the place felt like white clouds billowing over toward him from a smokestack aimed at his and Stewart's table. He experienced the fine sweat high on his forehead, and the miserable chill of constricted circulation in the tips of his fingers.

This was a full-scale anxiety attack usually reserved for

multifaceted nightmares. He wondered if his face was turning the color of salmon, and he actually clutched his throat to help the infuriating words get unclogged.

Allen and David never got off the boat. "And then . . . And then," David muttered and looked at Stewart pleadingly, as if his old friend could fill in the empty spaces of the grand tour.

"Are you all right, David?" Stewart asked, concern swimming in his voice and eyes.

And then . . . David was infuriated with himself but that just added an extra layer to the anxiety. He got terribly upset about being upset.

A bubbling personality? That was the way he had described himself sarcastically just a few minutes ago. Now David bubbled in front of Stewart.

Somewhere in there, words weighing upon his tongue, David realized that he didn't have to go down this road. He and Allen didn't have to ever leave the boat and Allen didn't have to die tonight by setting foot on the ground. David could slow down, have a glass of water, maybe decide to go on that grand linksland tour of Europe with Stewart, or discuss old times at Harvard.

Why, he could change the subject.

It felt like the attack went on for many minutes. All the colors of sophistication in the restaurant became dripping and primary. Even the food congealed before his eyes and a spot of spilled wine became bloodstained. But David was overpowered for only a few seconds, and then he got released from the grip; wrung out.

He felt his breath returning to normal. He cleared his throat, had a sip of water. "Jesus, sorry, Stewart."

"Okay, now?" Stewart asked, concerned.

"Fine, fine."

"God, you were gasping. I thought you were choking."

David took a last deep breath and felt in control now. He even managed a slight smile, a steady sip of wine. "I don't know what happened." He was back to his old understated self; his mild demeanor and good manners. "I couldn't breathe."

He had wanted to explain to Stewart; he had wanted to finally let it out a notch. But the grand tour was still too raw and had overwhelmed him—here in this French atmosphere, following on the heels of their talk about Elise. That troubled him later, the rawness of it, as he sat on the train back home from Penn Station. As did the look of concern and sympathy and bafflement in his dear friend's eyes.

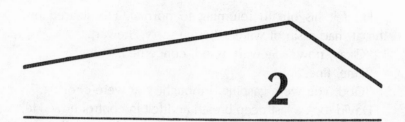

2

They sat in the library, and David asked casually, "By the way, have you heard from Emily lately?"

His father said nothing for a moment, then made a slight shrugging motion and replied, "Well, you know Emily, David, she'll come up when she's good and ready. I imagine, though, that she's tied down with work right now at her school. I wouldn't count on too much from her. These prep schools. She did promise to come up for a weekend soon, so we'll have that to look forward to. I think we'll get along."

The absence of any expression or emotion from his father surprised David. It was as if he had rehearsed warm reactions to David's anticipated questions about his daughter—"look forward to" indeed—even as he kept his distance, geographically and emotionally.

But more than that, David had the sense that Emily was part of his father's past, little more than a memory. The word "late" got stuck in David's mind. The late Emily. That was in his father's tone. Someone who had passed away but must still be dealt with at question time. The loose ends of a girl who is forgotten but not gone.

Emily's room was just off that wing of the house occupied by the maids and cook. The door was usually closed between them, but sometimes at night there was the sound, rising and lowering in pitch, of a television set—often with audience applause through the door.

Sunlight streamed in dusty shafts through the window. David opened the center drawer of her desk. He felt a guilty twinge about prying this way, but it didn't slow him down. He was worried about her. A year of weekly letters, sometimes twice a week, and then silence for months. Not a word. He wanted a clue to her and to why she had passed away from his father's mind, like a death in the family.

The maids had stuffed everything into the drawer—notebooks, small toys, a set of porcelain figurines, applications for summer jobs—but, most important, nearly a drawerful of photographs. They served as proof to David that the person whom he had come finally to appreciate only through letters received weekly from halfway around the world was indeed still living and breathing—and was, depending on the picture, involved, watchful, or irritated.

Irritated usually during the formal school pictures when a glare of sun seemed to be directly in her eyes. She stood in the back row because she was tall, but there was nothing awkward, nothing gangling; she just stood there, a tall girl with dark hair pulled back into a ponytail, a face slightly oval and strong-featured.

Yet David noticed something just a shade off balance about

her in the less formal pictures, and he spent some time look-ing at them before he discovered it was her eyes. Although they were not clearly present from the back row, they lent Emily's face the emphasis not of strength alone but of energy concentrated with great strength on a specific object—the camera perhaps, or the photographer's motions; whatever, her eyes kept up with it. The pictures in a way confirmed her letters: they were lucid and informed, but sometimes they took flight where David could not follow.

There was one snapshot—taken probably in her dorm room—of Emily and another girl, perhaps a roommate. Emily held the girl's arm, trying to keep her from leaving. Although his sister's expression was one of great pleasure, there was urgency in it also. She was making a point—a gleeful yet important one. What struck David was the other girl's expres-sion. Her face was turned in a blur toward Emily, but an image remained of great wariness and displeasure. The next frame, had there been one, would have the girl pulling out of his sister's grasp. Not serious, the snapshot, for the pleasure on his sister's face wouldn't have warranted it.

The last drawer was filled with papers. Most were school compositions, neatly folded, covered on the outside by teachers' comments. They were arranged in order, from the first year of prep school to the previous fall term. He was about to replace the stack in the drawer when he saw a small leather-bound pocket diary. He and his sister each received one as a present at New Year's but used them irregularly. Emily, however, had not missed a day for the previous year. Appointments, phone numbers—innocuous jottings to sum up the day. He noticed a number of men's names. David was surprised that she kept up the diary so faithfully, day in and day out. He did not associate such discipline with his sister.

Then there were two entries that caught his eye. One, the Friday after Thanksgiving: "Cocktails. Mrs. Talbot, etc." It had become a kind of family ritual, as long as David could remember, a cocktail party the day after Thanksgiving. Evidently that at least had continued despite his mother's relapse.

There was the other entry, on Monday of Christmas week —the last entry in the little diary: "Bergdorf's. Mrs. Talbot. The Plaza." And a series of exclamation marks; harsh slashes in red ink.

Cocktail party, Bergdorf's, the Plaza, Mrs. Talbot, slashes in red. David didn't try to make any connections, one entry to another.

Chantal Talbot. A first name that a child could hear the sound of reverberating in his head. One thing for certain: she was different. Chantal Talbot was so much exactly who she was that sometimes she reminded David of a gorgeously colored, extremely rare bird that had been set down among ducks.

Her husband had his "games." Name a game and Corky Talbot had played it or was about to play it, perhaps that very afternoon. Polo, golf, tennis, billiards, ice hockey, court tennis, squash, racquets, fox hunting. When he wasn't playing a game, he was watching one, and he insisted on watching it live. If there was a noteworthy sporting event, it didn't make any difference to Corky if it was being held on Long Island or Guam; he'd be there, front row.

It was a full life.

As a child David had not known what Corky and Chantal saw in each other, but probably it was money. The gorgeous bird arranged herself on a couch in their living room, leaning into conversation to capture every word, leaning out to observe the room crowded with guests. When others—particularly women—tried to sum up Chantal's beauty in a word, they referred always to her complexion, which had a pale almost transparent quality they prized highly. David couldn't have been less interested in that: as a child what he remembered best was her fingernails. They were so long they were like deep red pools; yet he never thought of them, or her even, as being shadowlike or threatening: rather, she was mysterious.

And over there stood Corky, the hearty, barrel-chested gamesman, season tickets stuffed into his too-scruffy blazer. His mind had been arrested somewhere in prep school, but it was a mind not without its third-form slynesses. Corky would pout if the day didn't break his way, but he wanted so little really. That's what always struck David: Corky just wanted to play games and watch them from the front row and call everybody "pal."

Chantal Talbot didn't quite fit. She moved in a society where people could go on and on about roast beef. David felt that she was some sort of visitor to Long Island, not quite a part of her surroundings. She was like someone from a book who had mistakenly wandered into real life and couldn't get out again, trapped in her high fashion colors, stranded amid the understatements, looking eager and mysterious at the same time.

But for his sister there was no love lost, no romance, no

mystery, no character who had stepped from a book. Emily detested Chantal Talbot, called her the Frog, or the Frog Princess, did a real nasty imitation of Chantal's "Ah . . . Dahveed." She criticized her clothes, her fingernails, her hair; turned Poor Corky—as Emily always referred to him—into a martyr burning at the marriage stake, caught in the intricate web of the fortune huntress.

Poor Corky.

Ah, Dahveed, Emily would whisper to David after parties, really drawing it out, with real hatred in her eyes, but not the hatred of a child. It was not transitory. This was a hatred of long standing, brooded over, added to, thickened, refined, allowed to mature and deepen. David could say with assurance that his sister's hatred was cherished.

But the hatred stopped abruptly with Chantal. Emily had a warm spot for Elise Morneau—Chantal's daughter, Corky's stepdaughter, David's girlfriend. It was as if Elise and Emily shared the same intense emotional wavelength of the outsider. In different ways, they both seemed to feel like immigrants in a new world.

David had half expected in those photographs at her prep school to see Emily ravaged somehow, as if some aging process had accelerated during the year he had been away. But there was only a kind of hardness about her. In the pictures Emily looked isolated from her schoolmates, as if she had wandered in from a different school.

There had been a whole year of letters, a mutual loneliness bridged tentatively. Emily had plunged into the state of Vietnam with the fervor of a discoverer in uncharted but enchanted waters. You know, it was a place that most people scarcely knew existed. She had pored over Vietnam, its oppressions and beauties, and turned it for David into a country with people and history, not a dangerous shithole. He sometimes wondered if perhaps Emily saw herself as oppressed and trod-upon by unfamiliar people with questionable motives. If that was the real steadiness, the one constant, of her character.

Ah, Dahveed, Emily would whisper, patting his cheek as if he were just the most precious thing. Such hatred.

David stood up and tucked his sister and Chantal Talbot and Corky safely back into the drawer, and left Emily's room.

Class, this is Elise Morneau. Elise is new to Long Island, and I want you to be especially nice to her. Elise lives with her family in Oyster Bay. She comes to us from Paris, France. Does anyone know where that is?

David had the distinct remembrance of "comes to us," because it sounded like a phrase from television, Ed Sullivan introducing an Albanian juggling act. Elise sat mercifully— from her point of view—at the back of the class. She had simply huge green eyes, and they took everything in as if they were scanning the vast dark skies.

"Hi," Elise said.

David must have been far away and alone with his soundless thoughts. She rode up behind him and said Hi and he jumped out of the way.

"God, I'm sorry," Elise exclaimed, but it was more like a question. "I didn't mean to scare you."

"Oh, hi," he said, trying to sound casual, returning from

someplace dark. He instantly wanted to make it clear: "You didn't scare me."

"I haven't seen you in a while," Elise said gently.

"No."

He felt a little annoyed with her; felt as if he had been discovered, though he couldn't remember what he had been thinking about. Jumping like that bothered him.

"If I get off, will you give me a leg up again?"

He misunderstood Elise's question as sexual. "Get off?" David asked.

"Or else I have to find a fence, or walk home. I don't think I can get back on him again."

Elise retracted the question by deed, because she slid off the huge chestnut promptly. "He likes to back away and make you hop after him with your foot in the stirrup. That's just *one* of his tricks. He's thrown me twice, and each time it was a two-mile hike back to the stables. God, was I mad . . . Look, I might as well be honest, David. I just couldn't call your house again. The reason I take this path is because I hope to meet up with you."

David walked beside her up the trail. "So what's on your mind?" he asked. It came out more harshly than he had intended.

"On my mind?" Elise asked, bewildered. "Gee. Nothing special. I just thought it would be nice to talk to you."

"I'm sorry I insulted your friend," David allowed warily. "Last month. Whenever it was. I felt very badly about that. I apologize."

"Accepted. How long have you been home now?" she asked.

"A couple of months, I guess."

"Any plans?"

Elise did an odd thing as she walked beside him, by bringing the chestnut's head nearer her so that it almost rested against her shoulder, as if for warmth.

"No, nothing definite yet."

She nodded nervously. "I'm at Barnard now. I decided I wanted to be in the city. I guess I wrote you that. I come out here once or twice a week to ride. I do it more to get fresh air than anything else. Did you get my letter?"

"Yes," David replied. "Thank you."

"You're welcome, I'm sure. You never wrote back."

"Well, with one thing and another . . ."

"These are the easy questions, David."

"Elise, I'm sorry, but what is it you came out here to talk to me about? Old times? Vietnam? My future?"

"If it's a multiple choice," Elise said quietly. "Old times."

"They were great," David said with a bitter tone that alarmed him. This wasn't going well. "Where would you like to begin?"

"Practically anywhere," Elise said, looking stunned. "After all, you were my boyfriend."

"Uh-huh."

She looked at him sharply. "Gosh, but now I see it's time to be on my way. Worst luck. Just when we were starting to have fun. I hate to ride off like this, but I'm getting cold."

"I'm sorry."

"In the absence of a fence, give me a leg up," she demanded abruptly.

David shrugged. "Sure."

"He's seventeen hands high, you know," Elise said, furious. "I don't know why I'm apologizing. First, you insult my friend by telling him he's got a funny name, then you make *me* feel like a stupid jerk. You know, David"—all this while she was gathering the reins and positioning herself to get on the horse, which was the largest hunter that David had ever seen, his first consciousness of its size; virtually borderline Clydesdale—"the little girl with the fractured English, she's gone."

The tight buttocks, the tango dance step arrested. David held her tiny boot for just an extra second—everything suddenly unalloyed, this winter-pure lust—before lifting Elise into the air with her own helpful little hop and her earthbound boot skipping along beside him. And then the way she sank into the saddle with a sigh and picked up the reins. Well, it had him smiling up at her inappropriately. This was not a complex matter like a family matter.

Elise, all gathered there above him. Her mouth made this expression like an old person's, transferred weirdly to a woman so lovely, a bit sucked in and her lips moving back and forth. She gave David just the most flickering glance, eyes brimming—no, not the schoolgirl with the saucer eyes.

He grabbed the reins. It was the pure sensation of grabbing and holding on to something. What a decision. Because in one second she would have been gone; by him, as in history.

"Just hold your horses," David said quietly to Elise, soothing the great chestnut hunter. The terrific muscular gathering ebbed slowly. The animal seemed to realize that it wasn't going anywhere, held so tightly by both of them. "Just hold your horses."

And now David knew exactly where he was, with a perfect clarity. The bare hill, with the spire of the Empire State Building in the immense flat distance to the west. The Long Island Expressway shining east and west. Post-and-rail fences wobbling across white fields. Dots of racing horses. A red bloodspot to the north. A driveway winding through miles of bare maples.

A black object glided slowly down from the bloodspot. David could almost hear the runners of the sleigh.

"Can we start all over again?" David asked tiredly, looking up at her. "I seem to have gotten off on the wrong foot." Thinking of the graceful length of her and his airy lifting.

"That's putting it mildly," she said, glistening mouth and eyes. "But I come this way often."

In the evenings, after supper in his mother's room, David would pick up a book from his room and go down to the library. His father would spend a little more time upstairs, then come down to join him.

The telephone rang. His father answered, said, "Just a moment please," then turned in his chair, with his hand over the receiver: "David, it's for you," adding, "A young lady, I believe."

If David had thought about it he would have taken the call in another room, but he didn't make any connection with the call until the phone was actually in his hands. He paused, holding the receiver, and his father went back to his book.

Jane said over the phone, "You didn't call me, David. I wanted to talk to you."

"I meant to call, really, but I've been busy." It was not just that he felt guilty about not calling her; he felt a kind of fear, as if an unbearable part of his past were summoning him.

"Oh, it's all right," she told him. "I have to keep reminding myself that we've never even met."

"We almost did," David said. "My last leave, before Allen and I left, but I guess something came up."

"I called mainly to invite you again."

His father stirred restlessly in his chair.

"How's the baby?" David asked, trying to steer the conversation away from this invitation looming; actually thinking of himself for a moment as calm, cool, collected. Unfortunately, it's not the future that's unpredictable; it's the past.

"Emily? Oh, she's fine. She's six months old now. I can't wait for you to see her. She looks just like Allen."

Emily. David hadn't known they'd named her Emily. That put him away. And the fact that she looked like Allen only increased his trepidation.

He held the phone away from his ear and stared at it as if he were grasping the entire concept of telecommunications for the first time in his life.

From approximately eight thousand miles away, his father took off his glasses and closed the book. *The Eustace Diamonds.* He stood up slowly, and David moved out of his way. His father said, *Well, good night, I'll see you tomorrow. Turn out all the lights.* And David said, *I will, good night.*

She said, "And then Allen mentioned your sister and I thought, well, I've always liked the name, so if it is a girl, which of course it won't be because Allen wants a boy . . . But mainly I liked the name."

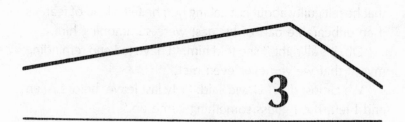

3

He sat on the train in the early evening, heading toward New York. The rush hour was over, but the car was full. There was frost on the window by his seat, and through the blur he could see streetlights and the red lights of slow-moving traffic.

It was necessary to change trains at Jamaica Station—from diesel to electric for the ride into New York. It always meant to David the end of Long Island and the beginning of the city. The train was late, and he waited among one of the widely spaced clusters of passengers. A cold wind blew across the tracks and under the blue station roofs toward the town. Several passengers stood sideways to it, hands in overcoat pockets or heavy fur coats, stamping their feet and blowing their breath in misty streams.

David separated from the group and moved to the edge of the platform. He leaned out over the darkened ravine dividing the platforms and peered hopefully down the track for a sign of light.

"I may be going to California in August," Jane had said

over the phone. "I have a cousin there, and I'll visit her for a while. It's warmer; most of my friends have gone out there."

He took a taxi downtown. The cab drove by a park with a high black iron fence around it. It was well lighted and David could see old people on benches; a wall of black coats and sturdy hats as heavy and permanent as somber statues. The cab turned into a dimly lighted street, drove a little way, then stopped. As he paid the driver David noticed the array of full garbage cans, most of them lidless, and garbage bags that had spilled over onto the sidewalk.

WE, THE UNDERSIGNED, WOULD LIKE TO
PROTEST THE RUDE, CRUEL AND INHUMAN
TREATMENT BY FEDERAL NARCOTICS AGENTS
AND THE POLICE DEPARTMENT OF THE CITY
OF NEW YORK. A MEETING TO ORGANIZE SUCH
A PROTEST WILL BE HELD ON . . .

The sign had been taped to the wall just inside the apartment building. It was illuminated by a single weak light bulb in the middle of the corridor, which cast its shadow on the rough yellow plaster of the walls. Just under the bold lettering was a long list of names handwritten in block letters.

David walked down the corridor and stood at the bottom of the stairwell beside a row of damaged mailboxes, waiting until his eyes adjusted to the darkness.

"The apartment is nice really," Jane had said. "It's getting there that's the problem."

He walked up the stairs. He heard a door open from floors above, then a girl's laugh. The girl said, "Oh no you don't," and there was the sound of running down the stairs, followed by laughter.

A male voice said, "When I catch you . . . ," but the rest was lost in a shout from the girl. He evidently caught up with her on the next landing for there was a brief scuffle. The girl said in a plaintive voice, "I won't do it again, I won't do it again," but the effect was ruined by their mingled laughter. Then David guessed she must have punched him. He said, "Shit," but she was down the stairs with a laugh. Running, she passed David at the next landing, paused at the stairs, turned to him and said, "Boo." Then her pursuer turned the corner and passed David without a glance—a tall man in a heavy navy coat; red hair, beard and mustache. They continued down the stairs and out the front door of the building.

David used matches to find her apartment. There was no light bulb on the third floor; only the filament remained in the socket.

He lit a match at one door and a dog barked. He moved on, farther away from the stairs. He found 3C, her apartment number, at the back of the landing, just off a short corridor. He rang the bell twice but there was no sound. He knocked on the door, then heard her say, "Just a minute. David, is that you?" from deep inside the apartment.

"Yes. No hurry," David said.

He thought that one evening wasn't too much for her to ask. One evening, one dinner—painless.

Jane opened the door. There was the briefest moment when her expression questioned him. The moment lodged in David's memory, as did the next, of delight and visible relief. Then she destroyed whatever notions he had had about formality or distance by holding him; the movement toward him almost involuntary, the pressure of her hands on his shoulders, pushing away the evening he had constructed in his mind. "This is very nice," he joked. "I appreciate the warm reception."

Jane smiled and said, "I'm glad you're here, David." She held him at arm's length, her eyes steady on his face. He thought there was something she expected from him, something that he was supposed to give her. He saw eagerness in her look, and something nervous and intense. "I'm glad you're here," Jane repeated, this time as if to herself, and released him.

She said, "You know, I haven't seen anyone quite so dignified in a long time."

"I've been looking forward to meeting you," David said with a smile. "I wanted to dress for the occasion."

There was a kind of script in his mind about how the evening would go—a certain way it would go, and then it would end neatly and with it the obligation. He wore a dark suit, as if to lend the occasion the extra formality of a somber ceremony carefully rehearsed. He felt a vague sense of agitation that things might not go as he had planned.

He looked around. The front door opened onto a corridor. Off it were kitchen, bedrooms and, through a doorway at the end, the living room. The kitchen was directly to his left, separated from the corridor by a curtain, open now. There were two small windows in the kitchen, but the darkness outside was not of night but of murkiness, thick and permanent. "The living room is much better," she said quickly. "I really haven't gotten to this part." She took his arm. "Come on, I'll get you a drink. I only got back from work a few minutes ago, so I haven't had time to clean up."

"I don't want to be any trouble," David told her. "I thought we might go out."

"No," she said firmly. "I want to test my cooking on you. You'll just have to make an effort to be polite, and *then* we'll go out."

"From the way you've set the table, it looks very special," David said. "I like the china."

"Actually," Jane said. "I've been taking a cooking course. I guess as more of a distraction than anything else."

He looked around. "By the way, where's the baby? . . . Where's Emily?"

"She's asleep in the bedroom. We can look in on her later, if you want."

"Fine. I'd like that."

Her appearance—especially her eyes—reminded him of soldiers he had seen. Their gaze settled on something and never left it—did not necessarily observe it, but never left it. She was under great strain: he had felt undercurrents of it when he had spoken to her on the phone. Now her every gesture seemed just a fraction speeded up.

"This is it," Jane said, with a touching tour-guide introduction to the living room; the underside of her wrist exposed. Allen, standing in line, had once held out his fatigue cap like a beggar's. "I don't know what to do about that space, by the record player. Something should go there. The desk is nice; Allen's mother gave me that."

"Yes, I like that. And you've got those big windows, so you must get a lot of light. Am I wrong, or is it very quiet?"

"Sometimes, but the people in the next apartment like to throw bottles at cats on the fire escape. Would you like a drink? I have scotch, beer, what else now . . ."

"Just a beer would be fine."

"I bought some wine for dinner," Jane said. "I got very confused at the store. The salesman was such a promoter. Anything less than ten dollars was an affront to France. I decided on a big bottle of something inexpensive. I don't know how good it is. We haven't gotten to the wine part of my course."

She returned to the kitchen. David took off his coat and put it on a chair. The living room was large and comfortable, with miscellaneous furniture: record player, bookcases, two floor lamps, a long red leather sofa that took up most of one wall. There were a dining room table with folding leaves, at which she had set two places, and a thick light-colored rug on the floor. At one end of the room was a small desk wedged into a space between the living room's two high windows. "What's out the window?" he asked, but already his eyes were on the bookcase.

"A garbage dump," she called. "It's not supposed to be, but everyone throws things down in it. I'll be there in a second. I just have to turn this."

"Take your time." More to himself than to her. "I'll just look through these books. Some of them look familiar."

On the shelf was a dog-eared collection of paperbacks. David took one down and looked at it. *The Good Soldier Schweik.* It was grimy and stained with sweat on the cover and through the first few pages.

David remembered wrapping Allen's books to send to her,

thinking she wouldn't know if he kept one; the one he held. It was odd how much it had bothered him—to keep it or not—but finally he had wrapped it along with the rest.

Her arms were folded tightly as if she were cold, her hands hidden. Outside the window he saw the blue glow of a television set from the next building. She was looking down now, absently scuffing the rug with her shoe. She asked, "Do you remember the letter you sent me?"

"Yes, sure." He put the book on the shelf.

"Did it take you a long time to write?"

"Yes," David said. "I remember I wanted to make it a good letter, and have you understand about Allen and what he meant to me."

"What *did* Allen mean to you, David?"

"Civilization," David answered, right off the top of his head. He briefly considered adding something—civilization and whatever he meant by that word—but let it ride.

It was okay. Jane nodded and turned away. "I wondered why you didn't call me when you got back. I waited for a long time, and I kept saying to myself that he must be back now—unless something happened. But it was good too, in a way . . . I called the second time and you never called me back, and I said, Well, that's that, I won't bother him again. But I did; I thought I'd give it one last try."

"I would have called you, I think," David said quietly. "It would have taken a while, but I would have called you. It's just that a lot of things have happened to me."

But he wasn't really sure that he ever would have called her. What he wanted to do was put his Army experience as far behind him as possible. He thought of the place of the

Army years as like a compartment in his mind: tangible as metal, locked; sturdy and impervious yet also somehow portable, so that the compartment could be pushed further backward until those years disappeared and a hazy blank space existed where they should have been.

She sat down on the sofa. She was wearing a white turtleneck sweater and a red skirt. Her hair was caught at the back and drawn off her forehead. She smoothed it with her hand, distracted. She was certainly the same girl as the one in the photograph that Allen had shown him long ago during basic training. The same girl of Allen's energy. But that lovely girl long ago, caught in a flash, didn't have a care in the world, or so it had seemed to David back then.

"It was a wonderful letter," she concluded.

"Thank you." He glanced back at the bookcase. "I was just thinking about Allen and how he loved to read. He read all the time, and he didn't like to see me without a book either. Said it would keep my brain from atrophying. If it hadn't been for him, maybe I'd have read comic books. It surprised me how many people over there read them. Naturally, I would have read only the *Classics Comics,*" David added with a smile. "Let them think I'm a snob, I don't care . . ."

At dinner she watched him intently. He said, "Very good, Jane. Really." And he was impressed with the effort she had put into this dinner—a rack of lamb that was delicious.

She looked pleased. "It *is* pretty good for a first time."

He was glad to see her relaxed. He had insisted on helping her, and she had said it was okay, she could do it herself, but had not protested when he helped bring in the food. She had stood for a moment looking at the table, but not as if it needed

79

anything extra; she had just stood back and looked at the whole scene of the table.

"Are you really going to California in June?" David asked.

"In August, I think," she said. "I really want to go."

"Don't you like the neighborhood?"

"Oh, it's not the neighborhood so much," Jane said. "I could live here."

"Are you still going to college?"

She nodded. "When I graduate I'll be able to get a better job. It's really important to me that I graduate in May." She looked thoughtful for a moment, then said softly, "I have this friend—he lives upstairs—and he knows some people in northern California. There're these communes, and the way he described them it really sounded ideal for the baby and me, at least for a while, until we get settled. I don't mean for good, David, but until I decide what I want to do. I do want to finish college, but I don't much want to live in the city if I can help it. Allen always talked about that kind of life."

"What about your cousin?" David asked.

"My cousin?"

"When you called, you said you had a cousin in California."

"Oh, yes, I do," she said. "It would be all right for a little while, but I'd have to find a place of my own after a couple of months."

He didn't think she had a cousin in California. He didn't think she knew what she wanted to do. He didn't want to offer advice, fearing that she would seize upon it—a lifesaver thrown to a person drowning. Suddenly he had that image of her—drowning, her hair floating like long grass.

"David, I must know everything about Allen." There was such intensity and avidity in her eyes. "Everything, so I can see what he saw and feel what he felt . . . This is very important to me . . . You're my only link to him."

People who want to know everything are like people who want to get away from it all. Sometimes when they get there, they don't want to be there; worse, it's a long way back to where they came from.

"Sure," David said slowly, drawing out the word. "I understand. Anything you want to know."

And he was surprised how easy it was, telling her. Ever since walking in the door of Jane's apartment, he had expected at some point to be overcome by the kind of anxiety attack—the gasping and throat-clutching—that had assaulted him in that French restaurant with his friend Stewart. It had scared him then, and now he kept monitoring himself for warning signs, testing his words, half expecting that at some point he would press the button of one particular magical word and the room would close in on him. But he felt quite calm with Jane. There was a sharing here.

He thought it would be a good idea to tell her about the baby first. Though an image did come to him just then, causing him to make a face as if he had just eaten something very sour; when the eyelids flutter—an image of a zipper closing over a fist.

Yes, the baby. That had been nice. Such a hot day, though. Allen and David were talking to some men just back from patrol. The men, dirty and tired, had caked mud up to their thighs. They all stood around a glistening water bag and gulped at the water as fast as their cups filled up.

God, and this is great, there was the smell of fresh-baked bread in the air; something wafted over from the nearby village. The smell was bread, the sound was hill-to-hill Beatles and when not the Beatles, it was Bob Dylan. David had read that morning in the Army newspaper that an ex-hog-cutter in the States had been arrested and accused of substituting sea water for salad oil in vats. He was being held on bail of forty-six million dollars.

The incongruities slayed you. Lieutenant Preston lifted the flap of the tent. He was their company commander, and a menace. Eagerness and paranoia fought for his soul. If you so much as met Lieutenant Joseph Preston's eyes—just looked at him—he would scream at the top of his lungs, "What the goddamn hell are you looking at?" He suffered from inferiority about his comparative shortness of stature, and wore elevator combat boots. That was the gossip. He wouldn't talk to you at all, not even to issue an order, unless he was physically higher than you were, so often it was necessary to follow him around in silence until he found a hillock, a box, or the back of a Jeep.

"Why don't we just build him a pitcher's mound?" Allen had asked in disgust. They both agreed that he should not be allowed to lead troops.

Lieutenant Preston blinked against the sudden light. He was holding a piece of paper. He summoned Allen over with a wave, and David accompanied Allen. Instead of walking toward the lieutenant, they walked toward where the lieutenant would *likely be* when he finally took the high ground; in this case, the back of his Jeep. So they all met at the Jeep.

Lieutenant Preston stood above them. He handed Allen

the piece of paper and said, "Congratulations, G.I.," as expected, stumbling right into the *wrong movie*. David uttered a regrettable sob of laughter.

This was their best day in Vietnam by far, and he shared it with Jane tonight. Lieutenant Preston making a beeline for the Jeep, Allen's comment about the pitcher's mound, the fresh-baked bread in the air, the Beatles, the salad-oil king stateside. Everything.

Allen looked at the paper. He took off his glasses. He said, "It's a girl," turned to David, "Hey, it's a girl. Would you believe that, Davey?" And David laughed. It was very beautiful, watching him. "I'll be damned," Allen said. "They say everything's fine. Jane's fine, baby's fine, everything's fine."

Allen looked down at the paper again, read the words aloud, shook his head. His face grew red—a face thin then, and stubbled with beard; bony.

David said, "I'm really happy for you." Allen's pleasure seemed so total.

Allen wandered away, looking down at the paper, looking up again, as if the words were just beginning to come clear to him.

That night, as they stood around organizing for patrol, Allen placed a flower in the barrel of his rifle. He cradled the rifle, with that flower sticking out, with a silly grin. After a few minutes he removed the flower. He held it in his hand, smelled it once, moved over to face David. He stood at attention. He said, "I'd like to present this to you," and stuck the flower into the barrel of David's rifle.

Allen informed David that there was a hill located somewhere on Long Island where Walt Whitman used to go to meditate. From that hill, Allen said, the poet could look south to the Atlantic Ocean and north to Long Island Sound. David insisted that that was impossible; no hill on Long Island was high enough to permit such long views. And certainly not around Huntington, where Whitman had been born. But Allen remained absolutely convinced that he had read somewhere of Whitman climbing a hill and seeing these two separate bodies of water across the flatlands of Long Island.

David and Allen went round and round about this goddamn hill. David got competitive about it because this was close to home, and he ought to know. Allen had a lot of teacher in him, and the prize student grew rebellious.

Finally, they just left it that when they got home they would go find this hill. Even though David didn't believe it existed, it came to exist for him over time with a remarkable fixity: hill at sunset, plains of Long Island lapping at its foot, twin shinings in the distance.

Jane liked this story.

He and Allen took a rest-and-recreation leave to Hong Kong. David was surprised how few soldiers took advantage of these leaves. It was as if they dug so deeply into their own weird little worlds that they refused to come out even when it was okay.

They were in a taxi, heading to the hotel from the airport. A boy darted into the street after something—a ball, a kite perhaps—and the car in front of their taxi hit and killed him. The boy seemed to sink under the car, grappling as if his hands were breaths. Screech of brakes, the taxi stopped, David leaned back in the seat next to Allen and thought, as appropriate banishment of the scene, *I've seen worse.*

Yet that damn accident, detail after detail, stayed with him and cropped up without warning and got linked with Allen's death. The kid took longer and longer to sink under the car, David took longer and longer to turn and make some joke about Lieutenant Preston or their mythical shared Whitman-esque hill. "Probably," David had once told Allen, "that hill is called Bridle Path Estates now. We'll have to ford swimming pools and hack our way through dense pachysandra to get to it. And *when* we get to it, we'll have a romantic view of Aqueduct Race Track."

Allen took longer and longer to trip the wire that shot up the mine that cut him in two—literally.

So this is what literally means.

Not *everything* for Jane tonight. Certainly not mines around the letters.

David stuck to the humorous and the painless and the bagless, left the husband dazed with joy at his firstborn; left the widow smiling as the two comic young men peered through spyglasses in search of water. David was oddly conscious that he was a lot like his father in his business suit; quite proper, making others reluctant to ask for details.

David glanced at his watch, finally. His discarded M-16 rifle blossomed with flower power for her. There was something he kept thinking about, something that Allen had once said; it kept recurring, nagging at him. "There was something Allen used to say when it was really bad sometimes," David told Jane. "He used to say that people are fragile." As if it were some monumental revelation, as if he had just stumbled upon this vital knowledge.

"I guess you had to have been there," David added apologetically. There would be no apotheosis for Allen, and he regretted that.

"Would you like to see the baby?" Jane asked.

"Sure."

She looked at him for a moment as if to make sure it was the truth. Then she got up. "I think you two should meet."

The bedroom was sparsely furnished. There were a bureau against the wall and a bed opposite with a colorful spread; really the only bit of color in the room. She whispered, "I've been meaning to get to this, but with work and everything . . ."

The crib was brand-new, an island in that spare room. The windows had shades and fading curtains. There were a few books in a small case set into the wall. The single overhead light bulb muted the room. David leaned over the crib, but he couldn't see the baby clearly; only a tuft of hair and tiny fists curled over the blanket edge. "I've read every baby book that's ever been written," Jane said.

"How old is she?"

"Six months."

He could make out the face now, as the baby moved slightly; veiny and soft but with a busy independent expression. He asked, "Does she cry a lot?"

"All the time. I've had practically everyone in the building to sit with her, but only once. She cries when I leave and stops when I get back, very pleased with herself."

David said, "It must be pretty hard for you, raising her alone."

Jane leaned against the crib, her arms folded. "Yes," she said. "After Allen was killed there were nights I'd wake up screaming. She kept my mind off a lot of things because she took up so much time. When I got home from work I'd have to take care of her. I like taking care of her."

He remained standing when Jane sat down on the couch in the living room. "What are your hours at the bookstore?" he asked.

"Oh, that," she sighed. "About eight-thirty to four-thirty. Sometimes more if I want to work overtime."

"When do you go to college?"

She looked at him in the same questioning way as when he had first come in. "Tuesday and Thursday."

"I see," David said, but he knew that he was going to let it pass.

"I'd like to see you again," Jane said. "And hear more about Allen. I don't want to be a bother, though."

He sat on the train after Jamaica, heading home. Earlier, the overhead lights had flickered once and gone out, but no one had made a move to change cars. A middle-aged couple in front of David, slightly drunk, began talking loudly. Finally, the woman, with gray-blue hair, fell asleep with her head on the man's shoulder. There were isolated men about the car, most of whom slept, their legs up on the seat. At each station the lights outside would briefly illuminate the car and cause them to stir. The woman with gray-blue hair snuggled closer to the man beside her. David watched the whole car from his position at the back near the window.

The passengers, the train itself, the newspaper on his lap, did not interest him. He kept balancing things in his mind: she was not all right, but maybe things would work out in California. He knew she would not call again, no matter what went wrong. He wouldn't be able to stand it if something happened, if there was something he could have done to help. He could see himself learning about it years later—that this entire thing had gone on, a whole struggle, and he had known nothing about it.

Responsibility, vulnerability—lives that were different from his own—and David did not exactly stumble over the fact that she was great-looking.

"I'm free most weekends," she had said. "And except when I go to school."

David killed Lieutenant Preston—his rifle on automatic, pumping rounds into him—while they were having a perfectly reasonable conversation about the war and how it should be fought.

Lieutenant Preston said a commander had to be cautious about how he committed his manpower. With the wisdom of a sage, the good lieutenant added, "Human life is precious."

This sentiment nearly brought David to tears.

They were sitting under a tree and conversing as equals. David clicked his rifle to automatic. It was a sunny day, so peacefully quiet it made him think of early Sunday mornings back home.

David told Lieutenant Preston how sorry he was that the lieutenant hadn't gotten into West Point. "It's a pity," David said politely, wishing these new M-16s had more firepower, wishing he could get his hands on a Czech-made AK-47 sometime; four hundred rounds a minute. "Because everybody in this company knows you have what it takes."

David opened fire and the bullets flung Lieutenant Preston against the tree, pinioning him up there as if he were slumping off hooks. The bullets turned his flesh inside out and ripped the bark off the tree.

David fired until one clip was spent and then flipped the clip and continued to fire; kept flipping and jamming. The flesh of the tree behind the lieutenant's living belt became coated and gleaming like a candied apple . . .

It was on the candied apple image that the nightmare always ended, and David stared up from his bed.

But he preferred his nightmare to those first moments of reality when he would awaken at some hour wrapped in a complete body sweat. At those times his thoughts were impinged upon by real events, which he couldn't shake for many minutes afterward.

The real events.

Allen died, the world exploded as the company penetrated into the ambush. Everything was green and smoky, punctuated by screams and trees bursting above them. Lieutenant Preston—that fucking idiot—and David were flung together briefly, alone together in the middle of this battle without a center. Lieutenant Preston had the gleam of a fanatic unleashed in his eyes and bounced in place in his elevator combat boots, quivering with whole lust—he who had led them down this foolish path. There had been no good reason for this operation. They went looking for trouble, and they found it.

"Don't you love it?" yelled the lieutenant. "Goddamn, this is what we came for."

David's best friend was dead somewhere out there, decomposing piece by piece.

The complicity finally made David raise his rifle. Something of David was reflected in those mad eyes, and something in David's eyes got reflected back to Lieutenant Preston as the world flew apart with explosions and calls for medics and whimpers into the sudden silences that came and went. A complicity. The man thought they were in this together.

The two of them alone, so David raised his rifle and took aim at the back of the lieutenant's head and fired. And the lieutenant's head whipped around—"What?" a terror in his eyes.

"Don't know," David shouted. "Something."

The lieutenant's still-living head whipped back around to find the source in all that impenetrable green. David, his protector, stood over him for a moment and then flung himself into the chaos, wading back into the heart of the ambush to search out what was left of his friend.

Chilled to the bone, still trembling days afterward when he thought how close the lieutenant had come. If there had been the slightest extra twitch or word or glance or blink; the merest extra gesture, one more psychotic question, David would have blown him up. A killer's heart was in him; that's what made his nightmare—with Lieutenant Preston nothing but pulp above the beltline and a benign Long Island maple tree bleeding and ripped—so much more preferable to wakefulness at some godless hour.

He hadn't had the nightmare for months and prayed this wasn't a taste of things to come. He didn't want to look forward to these scenes every night.

Things getting stirred up now—Jane and Allen and Lieutenant Preston.

But he called Jane a few days later. He needed to reach out to her. They began to see each other regularly, and his trips into the city became more frequent. He waited for the nightmare and the reality-nightmare to return on other nights—things stirred up now—but mercifully they didn't.

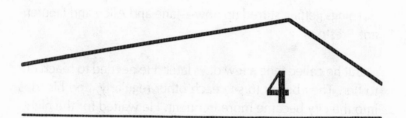

4

Her head rested in a hollow of pillows, her cheeks formed another hollow. She clasped a small silver-framed picture, clasping and unclasping it and tracing her fingers around the edges. She looked wide-eyed at the ceiling, her face the color of wet sand.

The picture was of herself at Emily's age; of a girl with blond hair that fell and curled below her shoulders, in the center of a plain settee with her hands folded on her lap, wearing a nightgown with frills at the neck so much like the one she wore now.

The whole expanse of bed was clean and white, blankets and sheets folded neatly. Pill vials stood in ranks on her bedtable. There were spots of snow on the lawn below the window, and the sun glanced off their crystals. Wet snow, perfect for throwing.

His mother shook her head. She clasped the picture, her lips moving. "Emily will be coming up soon, won't she? I'll plan a big dinner. I'll just call the school. She's studying so hard, poor thing. She keeps writing me about how competitive it is, how all the girls are in a panic about it . . . What's *wrong* with her? All I get are these letters. She never calls. She hasn't called since Christmas, and even then she was so distant. You like to have news of your children. Perhaps it's a phase. Who knows? . . ."

He always worried that he might come to see life as his mother did—in a kind of permanent retrospect, receding even as it was happening. He had listened to her stories, polished as ivory, as a child must, but had felt relieved when his obligation was over with and he could get away, get outside, get some fresh air. He wondered sometimes if his simple desire to get out of that musty bedroom led him to make bad decisions.

David watched the doctor arrive. Tall and dignified, in a heavy dark blue overcoat, the doctor got out of his car and paused for a moment to look up at the house. His thin lined face was without expression.

Downstairs in the front hall David heard him call his father's name, softly; as if the front hall, the house, was a mystery and web of entrances and exits; as if he hadn't been there a hundred times before.

His father came out of the library and met the doctor. They spoke in low tones for a moment then began to walk up the stairs. They paused once or twice to discuss the paintings hanging on the wall.

Each time David accompanied the doctor to his mother's room, there was that same procedure. The doctor, an elderly gentleman otherwise without pretense, would take a stance at one of the pictures, his bag close to his body and one finger outthrust theatrically at some minor point of composition.

David heard him now: "Now that's interesting, you see, just there. I do think he did the best horses. As I recall, this used to hang in the front parlor of your mother's house. I believe it was one of her favorites." David could see his father pacing along behind the doctor, hands behind his back, polite and deferential.

Down the corridor, their voices rising as they moved, jovial now as they neared her room, in the middle of a joke that would last through the door and linger on their faces: only a checkup, his father had said, except that this was Monday and his father had stayed home from work—something he never did. The door of his mother's room closed behind the voices, and David could hear nothing.

He picked up a book and went downstairs to the library. He sat in the chair by the bookcases, waiting, with the book on his lap. After a few minutes his father came downstairs. He stood for a moment at the door, looking tired and preoccupied. David wasn't sure whether to say something or just let his father look up and see him.

"How are things?" David asked, expecting anything—a joke, even a shrug and no answer.

"Fine, fine," his father murmured. "Doctor's in there now." He sat down in his chair. He did not move for a time but sat with his hand shading his eyes. Then he dropped his hand and looked blankly out the bay window. This lasted for the longest time and then his father stirred, sighed and reached for a book in the case.

When the doctor came down and wanted to speak to his

father alone, David went outside. It was a bright sunny day. He walked around the driveway occasionally kicking at the gravel, his hands in his pockets.

The doctor came out the front door. He seemed so preoccupied that David thought they might pass without speaking, but as he approached the car, he stopped. His face was hard and formal, his eyes, always so lively in that old face, were distant. He looked tired; his voice was soft, almost inaudible. "I have spoken to your father, David. I'm sure he will speak to you later. Your mother isn't getting enough care here. I have decided to put her in the hospital, where she will get very good care. I have told her that this is just for a checkup. I felt that the sooner we did this the better."

The doctor paused, and his face softened. He ran a hand through his white hair. "We felt that because of the nature of this . . . illness"—how the word floated—"no harm would be done by keeping her here. It might even have therapeutic value for her. We felt that with the necessary precautions . . ." The doctor shook his head and looked down at the gravel. "But we want her to have the very best care."

David nodded; then, for some reason thinking it was expected of him, he said, "All right."

"You've seen war," the doctor said. "Your father tells me."

"Yes."

"She has no insides," the doctor said, almost meditatively. "There's our problem."

David might have seen war, but he was enraged by the doctor's remark. What the hell happened to the old bedside manner that this man was so famous for? The song and dance to soften the blows? Why else did they hire this guy? He looked like one of those soap opera doctors on television.

No insides!

How do you think a person's insides are supposed to look after thirty years of twenty drinks a day? Like a newborn baby lamb's?

Without even asking, they come out of the box at you. You don't even have to ask them for their opinion anymore. They want to give you the truth like they're bringing the news from Ghent to Aix.

Walk it off, David thought. *Slow down.* You're bouncing around like you've got to take a piss.

God, *Ghent to Aix.* We're ten years old and it's the fifth grade.

The doctor opened the door of his car, slid his bag across the seat and got in. David remembered parties, large and small; voices and laughter rising in wave after wave to his room, glasses, tuxedoes and long dresses and perfume, the driveway full of lights glinting from the bright light at the front door. Mornings after he had come down to the living room, seen the naked glasses and bottles, the full ashtrays, and in his mind had filled the room all over again. Now David and his father would occupy the upper floors of the house, everything below covered in white linen—his sister gone, his mother gone—David himself in that enormous house.

One morning when he was ten years old his grandfather—his father's father—died. It was a Saturday in midwinter; so cold that he wasn't allowed out to play. He stood at the living room window and watched birds whirl around a feeder on the lawn.

The phone rang a few times, then stopped, and David guessed his father had answered it upstairs. He left the window and began to play around the living room with a football. He carried it with him constantly—a regulation professional football. He knew it would be only a matter of time before his hands grew large enough to hold it without support, but he had the idea that, just as a baseball glove had to be oiled, so a hand had to be molded.

The front door slammed, his parents walked hurriedly to the car. David wondered why his father was wearing his suit. He wondered briefly if today was some event he had forgotten.

Later, his father stood at the living room door. He said, "Here," smiling, and David threw him the ball. His father felt it for a moment and said it needed more air. He threw it back, David threw it back, his father threw it back. His father said, "Don't knock over your mother's china. There'll be hell." They threw it back and forth. David threw a perfect underhand spiral while his father regarded the ball warily. His father said: "Your grandfather died this morning." He said it matter-of-factly.

David didn't understand; the football needed air. He found himself nodding. His father looked so important in his suit that David nodded importantly, deeply, gravely, but his eyes were on the football. The game of catch slowed down, his father took seconds to throw it back. He held the football and looked at it thoughtfully, his lips tight and hard. Then he smiled and said to David, "Watch this. The old dipsy doo," turned a little, raised his knee, and the ball shot out straight and hard from behind his back, and David laughed so hard he barely caught it.

"Your sister in her room, David?" he asked. The old dipsy doo had moved him quickly to the door.

"I think so."

"Thank you," his father said.

His mother insisted on walking downstairs. David standing with the car door open, his father in front of her opening the front door, his mother bundled up with a thick black scarf around her neck, as if once out the door she would enter a winter storm. Instead there was crisp dazzling sunlight that made her blink.

A slow precarious operation, his mother grasping the banister downstairs, one foot at a time, pausing to rest, another foot now, very slow and easy. His father saying softly over and over, "Now take your time, take your time." It had been so long since David had seen her standing—a tall woman, and he at the car watching her as she came out the door.

She looked terrified. David's father at the door with his back turned, only the steps between her and the car. She took a vast step forward, that brought her right to the car. Alone, her deep eyes searching beyond the cars and driveway in quick birdlike movements. Then his father had her arm. He guided her down the steps and across the gravel to where David stood by the door. She put her hand on his arm, and he helped her into the station wagon. He sat in the back seat for the long ride into New York.

That afternoon he drove back from the hospital with his father. David wanted some kind of summing-up about the events of the day. His mother's situation caused him restless agony, yet he couldn't seem to get his emotions in order. He had a problem, because he wanted them to be like facts. His father dealt in facts. He feared that at some point he would be asked to be more *specific* about these floating emotions of loss and abandonment.

"What about this girl, David?" his father began, quite abruptly. Even though they had not exchanged a word since getting in the car, David felt as usual a weird sense—typical of fathers and sons—that they were changing the unspoken—furious and flurrying—subject.

"Jane."

"I guess so."

"What about her?"

"You seem to be seeing a great deal of her . . . David, I'm an old man and the shadows are lengthening, but I might be permitted a few liberties."

"Sure. What is it you want to know?"

"Well, who is she? Where's she from? What does she do? How did you meet her? You know, the usual questions."

"She lives in New York and works in a bookstore."

"A bookstore. My word. Is she by any chance—I hesitate to ask this—an intellectual?"

"No, I wouldn't go *that* far."

"Thank God. Tell me, how did you meet her?"

"She was the wife of a friend of mine in the Army."

"Was?"

"He was killed."

"I'm very sorry to hear that. Was he a sergeant too?"

"No, a private."

"Were you good friends?"

"Yes. He was my best friend in the Army."

"That's tragic, really . . . What's Jane like? Pretty?"

"Yes." He knew he wasn't being forthcoming.

"It's like pulling teeth."

"She has a baby, a little girl."

"I see."

"She really is alone. The bookstore brings in money, her husband's insurance left her some, and her parents give her a little, but it's no life."

"Perhaps she'd like to come out here some weekend."

"Maybe."

"Well, I think it would be fun for her. It will give them a chance for some fresh air, get out in the country. It would be nice to have a guest, a baby, the house being empty and all."

"Sure."

"By the way, just out of curiosity, what ever happened to Elise Morneau?"

"Why do you ask?"

"At one time you used to be quite an item."

"Elise is around. She lives in New York now and goes to Barnard. I see her once in a while when she comes out to Long Island. What can I tell you?"

"I didn't mean to put you on the defensive."

"You didn't put me on the defensive. Elise and I are just good friends."

"I'm not Walter Winchell, you know."

"Walter Winchell?"

"In other words, I don't mean to pry into your love life."

"Sure. I understand . . . My love life."

"Elise is a very nice girl." But David detected the relief in his father's voice.

"She really is."

"I gather this remains somewhat touchy. I'm sorry I brought it up."

"I don't mind."

"Fine, then. No more questions."

"Listen, I don't want to change the subject—"

"Certainly not, I'm sure."

"—but I was wondering, What have you heard from Emily lately?"

"Emily? Let me see. I hear from her prep school periodically to the effect that she is alive and well."

"I've decided to go down and visit her this weekend."

"Why? I wonder. All that long drive. It hardly seems worth it."

"I haven't heard from her in a long time, and I'd like to see how she is."

"As you wish."

His father shrugged. It was always the same: whenever he mentioned Emily, David got the sense from his father of irrevocable decisions made, emotions drained.

He had received a letter from Emily. Confused, rambling, bizarre. He thought of a girl with wild hair. She was gushy sometimes, incessant about Vietnam, yet kept returning with venomous anger to the unpardonable fact.

David didn't see what was so unpardonable. Then again it

had never occurred to him that Emily was unaware of the love affair between his father and Chantal Talbot; the duration of which could now be measured in decades. Everyone knew, he thought, except possibly the bloated Corky himself, who had his games.

Growing up, David and Elise talked about the affair all the time; it was the most terrific shared thing; the secret of the secret. They both found it instructive, the two little plotters, to observe their parents' exquisite minuets of discretion. It drew them closer. Also, the ongoing love affair kind of humanized his father. It weakened or at least blurred his careful image.

David managed to work up limited compassion for his mother and Poor Corky. The problem was that his mother had spent a lot of time in storage during David's wonder years. As for Corky, he could most often be found in places like South Bend, Indiana—getting down, or was it up, for the big one that decided it all.

Perhaps Emily knew about the affair on one level but didn't want to acknowledge it on another. Even so, this was hardly news to make worlds collide. David would have thought that Emily was above all that—the snideness and anger.

Well—it occurred to him briefly—maybe she *is* above all that. This whole affair between her father and Chantal Talbot might be nothing more than a sideshow for Emily; in Corky's terms, a tune-up for the main event that was taking place at another venue. If only he knew what she was driving at.

Whatever, it was a very strange letter.

There had been the cocktail party on the Friday after Thanksgiving. "The Ritual." Emily standing in for her indisposed mother, who had insisted that the show must go on.

"A procession of guests up to The Bedroom for the briefest look-in." The contrast between "the jangle down below and the hushed atmosphere upstairs."

His mother actually enjoyed this annual party, David knew. Its inevitability provided time for rehearsal, diminishing for her the social agony of just being in a populated room.

Emily *"standing in."* She rehearsed her own performance "like some movie star, searching stores for just the thing," settling finally upon "the Lord & Taylor look."

She must have been a knockout, David thought. All she lacked was a fur coat. Chantal Talbot had a dazzling fur coat. *"Think of the animals killed to make that coat,"* Emily scrawled, using her reddest pen.

Where was Corky Talbot in all this, David wondered—the husband? Emily didn't mention "Poor Corky" in her letter, but David knew. It was Thanksgiving week. You had the Giants and the Rangers and the Knicks, not to mention the East Coast college basketball and football teams.

David pictured Corky, far from cocktail party and wife, beaming down upon rink or court or playing field, red-faced in the artificial light. He saw Corky as a caricature sitting in a raccoon coat, waving a school pennant. Utterly happy—while back on Long Island a teenager "lingered sultrily," ten years ahead of her time, and the exotic wife was helped into her fur coat.

Chantal Talbot "whirled in the light of the front hall." Her coat had a ruffled, almost living texture. Emily "folded my arms and watched, tilting against the wall. The corridor leading from the living room to the front hall might have been the dimly lit street of a red-light district."

This moment that occurred: an adjustment by her father of the collar, a long kiss, Chantal's black, glistening hair sweeping across "the animal fur." Then she seemed to "slink out of the house like some low-slung ferret released to the night."

David felt envious of Corky Talbot, rooting away in one of his stadiums on that Friday night after Thanksgiving. You won, you lost, you rooted, you went home at the end of the game, and the next day began and you went out to play again. Life was all squares and circles and rectangles; green or hard or icy underfoot.

Corky Talbot stood up in his raccoon coat, waving his pennant rapturously. Emily "turned in the corridor and headed for the living room." She moved back into the voices, leaving the two "middle-aged lovebirds" to their own devices; ruffling and patting and then slinking away.

"This is exactly the kind of unprincipled and immoral thing that American soldiers are doing in Vietnam at this very moment," Emily wrote. "Killing a defenseless people with their bombs and bazookas." She had underlined the word bazookas, probably because of its sound. *"This has nothing to do with individual heroics,"* she added—too hastily—perhaps aware that she had included her brother in the saturation bombing.

Sable coats and Vietnam—this was the worst analogy David had ever heard.

Emily sounded exhausted when she got to the big scene. Red writing sloped downward. David wondered if the dawn followed the night in this letter; first the night thoughts and then the lucidity of dawn among Styrofoam coffee cups and cigarette ashes. He pictured Emily waking up in the morning at her school; the day soiled already just by her eyes' falling upon different objects and ruining them.

It was Christmas week then, and Emily was shopping in New York with a school friend, Liz Chase. They stepped out of Bergdorf's onto Fifth Avenue, and "the crowds seemed to slither and pour down upon us on the sidewalk from some mysterious, endless source." Pushing against the tide, she and Liz walked along Fifth toward Rumpelmayer's on Central Park South, "for tea, for hot chocolate, for just a place to sit down."

With *"both of my parents' presents in my shopping bag,"* with the whole prospect of Christmas vacation before her. They were going for hot chocolate, a couple of school chums, but Emily could "go anywhere in this city and buy a drink."

She could already taste the chocolate; she could almost hear herself and Liz giggling, though "Liz is a follower and has a horsey laugh—she's inbred but gorgeous." Yet some of Liz's "ga-ga amazement" at Christmas New York had rubbed off on Emily, though Emily was "tempted to drop off Liz at F.A.O. Schwarz and let her play among the toys all afternoon."

As the "tour guide" for Liz, Emily felt "worldly, yet with something of the Christmas spirit borne in by the city." She felt that she could "play it any way I liked." She could stand back and observe herself "giggling pink-cheeked" at Rumpelmayer's over her latest "schoolgirl crushes," sharing "normal confidences" with her chum and breaking up. She felt that her "whole day should have a musical accompaniment."

Right at Fifty-ninth Street and Fifth Avenue, she saw "the fur coat slink out of the Plaza." The doorman waved, the limousine pulled up. The elegant, gray-haired stranger leaned down to kiss Chantal Talbot and the door closed and the limousine pulled away, black and shiny in the "shocking winter light." The gray-haired stranger, tall and slim in his Chesterfield, "hunched against the seeping of the cold," promptly turned north toward Central Park.

"Fun." That was the word Emily was left with. "You don't associate him with fun." In the thirty seconds it took them to come out the door, wait for the limousine, kiss, depart, she had the sense of "there being just the two of them," with their dual pasts, presents and futures; their exclusive histories. Her father was a stranger because he had on "a private face," and every gesture he made from smile to kiss to brisk walk was "new and newly linked, so that his entire coordination seemed different."

It was possible that had Emily not seen that fur coat—"you couldn't miss those goddamn dead animals"—she would never have noticed him at all. She would have set off for Rumpelmayer's *"in all my innocence."* Which she and Liz never made, by the way, "much to Liz's disappointment." They found a hotel bar along Central Park South, "dimly lit and nearly deserted."

That was the extent of Emily's letter. The last section contained just the facts of her Christmas week afternoon in New York, the chance encounter with her father and Chantal Talbot. It was as if these bare facts alone were supposed to carry so much weight that they needed no amplification.

Emily mailed the letter but either forgot or just didn't bother to sign it.

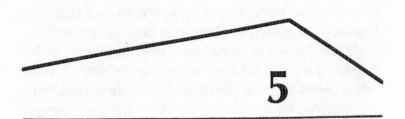

5

David left that Friday for Virginia and his sister. There was something pleasant about driving away. The car became chilly as it grew darker, and the chill worked its way through his sweater and made him alert. Several times he thought about turning on the heater, but that would have spoiled the mood. He enjoyed the simple task of driving.

Outside of Washington he turned on the radio. He located a familiar station from Savannah, Georgia. It played country music night and day and brought back memories of the long time he had spent at Fort Stewart, that large post sixty miles west of Savannah where he had trained. The disc jockey took the music seriously and always began his show with a song by the "late great" Jim Reeves or Patsy Cline.

What had ever possessed him to join the Army? he wondered, even though it was a little late in the day for regrets. He could have joined the Peace Corps instead, worked for a company for a year, hitchhiked around Europe, seen California. All his reasons were so distant and trivial now, but at the time they had been important. Now it seemed as if some impostor had made the momentous decision for him.

He saw himself as he had been then, just before he had broken up with Elise. A long summer before him, a June and July of debutante parties on Long Island, often three or four in a week. Waiting up for the scrambled eggs and sausages, driving home at dawn.

One night in particular. He stood by a library window in the hazy dawn and stirred his drink. A girl—not Elise—had begun a routine of standard questions, her face a positive tic of interest, as they whirled under the tent across the wooden dance floor—through that common area of gossip toward what David knew, as he felt himself actually brace for it, was thin air. His future. "I don't know," he had said.

A couple of small things made him decisive, and then Elise was gone. A young man with straight brown hair and glasses sat in a heavy leather chair in the library of a large house. He was covered with vomit, chin to crotch in it, his glasses askew on his face—stained—and his hands upraised and beseeching.

At the same party David stood next to the dance floor. He became aware of a row of tuxedoes beside him. The black row had a common interest: a pair of bright brown shoes far across the dance floor. David glanced back and forth, from the row of black to the brown shoes—loafers they were, scuffed, danced in by a short oblivious young man with long dark hair; his partner a lovely blond girl in blue satin. They had carved a space for themselves out of one small corner of the dance floor. Sometimes they danced in close embrace, sometimes yards apart, eyes half closed, heads nodding to the beat.

The brown shoes glared. Two young men of the row—each with a casual shock of dark hair slanting over the eye, hand in pocket, shiny black slipper outthrust—looked at each other. It was, that look, merciless and direct, but confident also—as if bound in some distant unknowable way to have an effect on that boy and girl dancing in the corner. David suddenly didn't want to have any part of these people. He was surprised more than anything by his own surprise. It was as if he were giving up a part of himself, a part of his heritage, by stepping back and away from them.

And then over the following days it became less important to him what he did than that he just did *something*. His grades had slipped at Harvard, he'd been drifting. Most of all he was sick of his own uncertainty. It had not occurred to him, long ago in 1963—way back then—that he might wind up in a bag.

Traffic thinned, roads narrowed, he pulled over once or twice to check his map after Washington. He peered at the wavy black lines that branched from the thick red road toward the heart of the state.

The closer he came to the school the more concerned he became that seeing Emily would prove anything. There were gaps and silences and subtleties that he didn't understand. She hadn't come home. His father got annoyed whenever David asked about her. She had written him weekly letters for an entire year, and then silence. She didn't write and she didn't call.

The school was larger than he had expected. It seemed to stretch far beyond the cluster of red brick buildings just off the main road. Pathways cut through rolling lawns, and playing fields were just visible through the trees. In the distance he heard the shouts of a game in progress.

He parked his Chevy II next to the unimposing white chapel, directly across from a sign on an ivied brick building: business office. He asked a girl, who came by on the sidewalk carrying books and a clipboard, directions to his sister's dormitory. She indicated a path that cut across the lawn and disappeared into the woods. The girl was tall and blond, and though it was a warm day, she wore a red cardigan. She held her books tightly, as if carrying them on an errand.

"Are you a friend of Emily Winant's?" David asked.

"She's in a few of my classes," the girl said. "She's very bright, you know." There was some hesitance in her voice. She began to edge away. "Just up that path. It's the nicest dorm actually. She has a room to herself."

"I just came down for the day to see her," David told the girl. "I wrote her I was coming."

"That's sweet."

David walked up the flagstone path, bordered by a well-kept lawn. The sun glinted off the stained-glass windows and the cross atop the white chapel. The path turned to dirt as it entered a wooded grove. The campus behind him, its cluster of ivied brick buildings—other structures just visible through the trees beyond—was deserted.

The path opened onto the dormitory. The grass around it was sparse and newly growing, and off to one side were stacks of wood half covered by a tarpaulin. The dormitory looked solid and unreceptive. It seemed closed to the outside clearing, woods, school, and to the sun. David had an impression suddenly of cubbyholes and mirrors and faces tilted this way and that.

He walked around to the side of the building and encountered two girls, one reclining on a wood-slat lawn chair, the other sitting on a cinder block that served as doorstep. A portable radio played loudly between them. The door itself looked formidable.

The girl in the chair glanced at David and looked away casually. Her hand crept to her hair and smoothed a wayward strand. Then she arched her neck and looked up at him. She said, "Yes?" in a tone that mixed surprise and arrogance. David realized that he had seen her somewhere before, and then he saw the snapshot and his sister gleeful and the girl trying to pull out of her grasp, twisting toward the camera, blurred face and hands twisting. He asked for Emily.

"I think she's at the library," said the girl from the steps and stood up. She was short and heavy with straw-blond hair, pigtails, and a wide freckled face, open and friendly. She put out her hand. "I'm Katie Owings, and this"—she put special, almost contemptuous emphasis on "this"—"is Brenda Dubell. The well-known socialite." The other girl looked away abruptly.

When they were out of earshot, Katie said, "Brenda is dumb," casually, as she bent down to pick up a smooth stone from the path. "And *such* an unfortunate name. That's what breaks your heart."

"Are you a friend of Emily's?"

Katie nodded. "I'm her best friend." She juggled the stone

from hand to hand. "You're not what I expected," she said. "At all. I was expecting a wild man."

"Does Emily have many friends?" he asked.

"I'm about it."

"Why's that?"

"Everyone thinks she's some kind of bomb about to explode, and they want to be as far away as possible. I don't, though. I want to watch the whole thing."

"How do you mean? Does she break a lot of rules?"

He would have felt greatly relieved by simple rule-breaking.

"Well, that's certainly one factor," Katie said with a nod. "Among many. I think sometime the keepers are going to come up with a charge like 'general obstruction to business as usual.' "

"What exactly *does* she do?"

Katie looked at David directly for a long moment, as if to size him up. She said quietly, "Look, this term we've had two attempted suicides and one successful one—if successful is the word. We have girls who don't go outside, girls who refuse to eat anything, girls who puke up everything they eat. We have arsonists, kleptomaniacs, drug addicts and prostitutes. It's a very special little world here," Katie Owings said grimly. "The thing about Emily is that she doesn't take anything for granted. That's scary, you know. She's terribly aggressive, but she's not a bully. She's—graceful"—Katie paused—"I mean, don't you think?"

"I just don't know her well enough," David replied. "Until I went to Vietnam, we'd pretty much gone our separate ways."

The library stood at the crest of a short hill. It was a large building of gray stone, with a white cupola at the top. The campus spread out below it, brick and ivy, dark roads, white spire of the chapel in the distance. From this height David could see the playing fields: baseball cage, white goal posts, and darting figures framed by a small audience. The leafless branches of the tallest trees gave each figure—base runners, underhand pitcher, shifting infield—a jerky motion, like an old silent film.

Katie was saying, "Well, she's in there somewhere. I'll leave you here." She put out her hand, and David took the firm grip. "Glad to have met you, David."

"Maybe Emily and I can stop by the dormitory later," David said. "We can go have lunch somewhere."

"Sure, if she's lunching this week." Katie paused, looking at him. "Something's killing her. Dunno what it is, but it's eating her alive. Do *you* know what it is?"

"No," David said, alarmed. "How do you mean, killing her?"

"That's an exaggeration," Katie said quickly. She put out her hands as if to block his negative thought waves. "I tend to exaggerate. I don't want to upset you. I just meant that something's on her mind."

"Well, that's why I'm here," David told her. "To find out what's on her mind."

"When you do, let me know," Katie said. "See you."

David watched her as she walked down the hill, strong back and thick legs, until she got to the sidewalk and disappeared among the trees.

He turned and walked up the wide steps of the library. He

entered through the heavy oak door and found himself inside
a large room. A display case in the center held biblical manu-
scripts under glass—tall florid Latinate writing. There were
oblong tables of thick rustic wood around the room, and stern
uncomfortable chairs. Shafts of sunlight from small skylights
dappled the hard furniture and the walls of books. There was
not a sound in the library. He stood for a few moments
looking at the books in the display case.

From behind him a voice said, "Hello, David."

He turned and Emily stood in a doorway that led off the
main room. She was smiling at him, but not at his surprise.
She held a yellow pencil in her hand. She said, "I heard
someone come in. I thought it was you."

She said it matter-of-factly; she did not move.

For a moment David was flustered. He said, "Emily." It
seemed to echo in that large room.

"Nice to see you," she said with an absence of inflection
that astonished him.

Her eyes were distant and cloudy, sleepless bruises under
them, and still she did not move.

Almost as an apology, David told her, "I just wanted to see
how you were. I know on the phone you said you were busy.
That's okay."

"I'm working on this term paper and pressed for time."

"Sure." David put his hands on the glass of the display
case. "I have to be getting back early, anyway." The impor-
tance of his visit slipped away then.

"Let's sit down over here," Emily said, with a formal gesture toward the stern table, the uncomfortable chair. "We
have the room to ourselves."

He moved to the chair. Emily's hand touched his jacket lightly, a dart of white that drew back almost involuntary; and she sat down primly across from him. She sat straight up in the chair with her hands folded in her lap.

"I thought you were having trouble," David said. "That's why I came down."

"Trouble?" she asked and looked surprised, as if nothing could have been further from the truth; further from the composition of reality.

"I had the feeling something was bothering you. You haven't been home, haven't called, and then you wrote me this strange letter last week. All about Chantal Talbot and Dad. Didn't you know about them?"

"Sure," she said distractedly. "I knew."

Emily studied the shelves of books beside her. David wondered how she could remain so placid and motionless.

"So I wondered what was going on. If you're having problems, maybe I can help."

He was speaking some imcomprehensible foreign language to her. Not a word was getting through.

"There's work to be done," Emily said distantly. "It is very competitive here, and I want to get into a good college."

David muttered, "Oh, sure."

Her eyes seemed hollow. She leaned back without expression. They sat in silence for a moment. Emily sat composed and erect in her chair—a tall pale girl with an attentive ladylike expression.

He tried again. "I was just thinking about a letter you sent me in Vietnam. You told me about the headmistress, and how you wondered why she'd never married. Do you remember that?"

"No," Emily said.

One more time, David thought. "You decided she'd had this love affair in her youth, and her lover was an aviator. You pictured him with a silk scarf. I really liked that—an aviator."

"He was probably a botanist."

"Sure," David said. "He could have been anything."

"Including a cliché," Emily snapped.

She made an odd motion with her hand. She moved it down from forehead to chin, as if slowly pulling a shade. "I enjoyed writing the letters, though . . . Look, there is this paper to do."

"You must think I came down here for the fucking drive. I came down here to see *you.*"

"And that's why I feel just terrible," Emily said quietly. "You came all the way down here for nothing."

"I thought we could talk. I guess not. You don't seem to want to talk."

"No, I don't," Emily said firmly.

He had to make contact somehow. "It's been sort of a shock getting home. I can't seem to get back in the swing of things."

This was not a phrase—"swing of things"—that he could recall ever using in his life. He had once seen a movie on "The Early Show" featuring Tommy and Jimmy Dorsey; another one starring Bob Crosby and his band, the Bobcats. Was it the Bobcats? Trivialities of his childhood dislodged and floated up like bubbles from the helmet of an undersea diver.

"You've always felt so *responsible,*" Emily said distantly. "That's what amazes me. Why, as if you could save us all."

"Maybe . . . Okay . . . That's a problem I have," David acknowledged.

"So touching and childlike. And godlike, arranging everybody the way you'd like them to be."

"Yes, it does get tiring." The image of a one-armed paperhanger came to mind suddenly and David smiled unexpectedly.

"*Poteris modo velis,*" Emily declared. "You can if you will. That's our school motto."

"Of *course,*" David said. "You can if you will." He bounced the flat of his hand gently off his forehead, eureka-like. "How stupid of me."

"What?" Emily asked suspiciously, tilting her head a little to get a better angle on him.

"Here I've been seeking wisdom and all along it was printed on the front page of your alumnae directory. *Poteris modo velis.*"

"You should get on with your life and not bother with my problems."

"I'd like to."

Emily shrugged. "As long as you're here," she said, making it sound like a statement all by itself, "I want you to understand something. And then I want you to *go.*"

"I just got here, for God's sake," David protested. "I thought we'd go out and have a few drinks, lunch, drive around, talk."

Just the tiniest flicker of life. "Are you happy?" Emily asked, and really it was so pathetic.

"I'm happier tlian you are," David answered truthfully. "I'm glad to see you. It's spring. Anyway, I just met your friend Katie. We can bring her along if it makes you feel any better. I don't care."

"Katie idolizes me. I think I've disappointed her. It's a terrible thing when you let people down. I want to make it clear I profoundly regret what happened to those horses."

"Oh," David sighed. "The horses."

"I'd give anything if it hadn't happened. *Anything.*"

"Emily, that was two years ago. It was an accident. Listen, a couple of months ago I was riding around with old Roger Jepson in his one-horse sleigh, and even he said it was an accident. And they were *his* horses, for God's sake. It was just a tragic accident."

"If it was just a tragic accident, why have I been condemned to outer darkness?"

"Who condemned you?"

"My father."

"*Outer darkness?* Jesus, a little angry maybe."

"Who gave him the right to pass judgment?" Emily demanded bitterly.

"Judgment on what?"

She wasn't listening. "His life hasn't been so totally above reproach that he can judge from on high."

"What does that have to do with anything?" David asked.

"You'll see," Emily declared, nodding vigorously as if one of her thoughts were agreeing with another.

"See what?" David asked.

She seemed to gather herself. She leaned forward, looking

directly at him, with her fists clenched—the intensity in that ornate library.

"I am not like you!" Emily exclaimed fiercely.

"No," David said, not sure if he was agreeing with her or just humoring her; not even sure if she meant him directly.

And then she leaned back in her chair, and at once her expression got replaced with the same eerie serenity as when he had first walked in.

"As long as you're here," she said calmly, "I wanted to make it clear about the horses."

"It's clear," David said.

"My profound regrets."

"Fine. Now can we have lunch?"

If I can just get her out of this goddamn library, he thought. *It's like her home territory.*

"Please go," Emily said briskly. She stood up and thrust out her hand with a kind of bold professionalism.

"Go?" David asked, baffled. But he *did* take her hand, almost as a reflex of politeness.

"Thank you for coming."

He felt as if an interview, not a conversation, had just concluded.

David had no intention of leaving. After a moment Emily simply turned away from him and walked abruptly out a side door of the library. Just was gone.

"Emily," David called, but then he heard his own deepened vaulted voice, newly amplified, reverberating, rescuing. It mocked him savagely.

"Em—" and he stopped and said no more.

David left the library and returned to Emily's dormitory, where he located Katie Owings, his sister's best friend. They drove into the small Virginia town near the prep school and had lunch in a booth at the town's only restaurant, which was little more than a coffee shop.

David told Katie—though he wasn't sure why—about this Mormon kid from Idaho, hardly more than eighteen years old, who had trained with him at Fort Stewart, Georgia. Their first day on the base, a black master sergeant in charge of the barracks gave the Mormon kid an order.

The Mormon kid told him, "I don't take orders from animals."

The black master sergeant waited a beat and asked quietly, "What did you say?"

And the Mormon kid repeated, "I don't take orders from animals."

"That's what I thought you said." It took half the barracks to pull the black master sergeant off the Mormon.

David told Katie, "I still don't know how that Mormon kid got all the way through basic training without taking an order from a black man. But he turned out to be a good kid once he got beaten to a pulp."

"You liked the Army." Katie bummed another one of his cigarettes, a Raleigh Plain End with the coupons on the back. Collect enough coupons, you get your own coffin.

"I liked the control," David explained. "I liked knowing what to expect and what was expected of you. I could have done without the rest . . . They don't let you smoke at this school, I gather."

"It doesn't stop anyone. You just worry about cross ventilation."

"Strict school?"

"Yeah, the last of its kind. That's why everybody's so messed up."

"Have they got anybody who can help, say, if someone's messed up?"

"It's called Expulsion," Katie said flatly. "That's all the help we get. Some old geezer drops by once a week, gives out aspirin if you've got cramps, sleeps on his examination table. For the most expensive prep school in the United States, we're not exactly leaping into the twentieth century."

Katie ordered another cheeseburger and another Coke. "I've got this weight problem," she told him. "You may have noticed. Emily you know's gotten to be quite the vegetarian. She won't even look at a cheeseburger. Sometimes we come in here and I have to eat for two. She asks me how can you eat the flesh of dead animals and I say hey, no problem. Do you know the single greatest question in the English language?"

David shook his head, feeling almost relaxed. You didn't have to extract life from Katie: she would tell you the story of her life in detail at the drop of a hat. She had human, understandable, down-to-earth, butterfat problems. Something you could get your hands on, so to speak. Not all this wispy, subtle, mystery crap that tired you out.

Katie wouldn't just walk out on you.

"You're not going to eat that?"

"Eat what?"

Katie sighed. "No, no, no. That's the single greatest question: You're not going to eat that?"

"Ah," David said and smiled.

"He smiles," Katie said. "When I first saw you, I thought you'd come to foreclose on the dormitory . . . Say, do you mind if I have another one of these? This is a real cigarette, boy. Have you got more somewhere? I don't want to take your last one if this is your last one."

"Go ahead. I've got more in the car."

"Do you know you chain-smoke?"

"Yes."

"How many packs of cigarettes do you smoke a day?"

"About three."

"Jesus Christ!" Katie exclaimed. "Are you a very nervous person?"

"So I've been told."

"I can see you're the type who is uncomfortable with questions of a personal nature," Katie told him, formally but not stiffly. "Actually, it's the strong, silent types who race Katie's motor." She seemed deep in thought for a moment. "Do you save the coupons?"

David shook his head.

"I think I probably would," Katie mused. "Do you know the four greatest words in the English language?"

"No."

"All you can eat."

David laughed, watching her light up her Raleigh.

"They have a great deep-dish apple pie here," Katie told him hopefully.

"Sounds good," David said, even though he wasn't hungry.

"With a scoop of vanilla ice cream. Frankly, they can hold the pie and just bring on the ice cream."

Katie's second cheeseburger arrived and she actually sighed with pleasure. Between bites she said, "I'm a great field hockey player, probably the best the school's ever had. The coach doesn't let me drink any water after practice. What do you think of that?"

"Why not?"

"Because of my weight problem. She doesn't want me bloating up."

"Your coach is nuts."

Katie chomped into a grouping of french fries that sprouted from her fist. "What really annoys me is she doesn't say I'm overweight or too fat. She always says 'obese.' That drives me up the wall. 'Katie, what *are* we going to do about your obesity?' Like I have a medical problem, like it's all real clinical. My biggest problem is cheeseburgers and deep-dish apple pie."

"In Vietnam I lost more men to kidney stones than to any enemy. Your coach is nuts."

"Kidney stones?"

"They can be caused by dehydration. You go down like a shot and beg for mercy. So drink up."

"I thought so!" Katie nodded vigorously. "See, that's what I mean. This school has not entered the twentieth century. I wouldn't be surprised if we had an outbreak of cholera. We're talking medieval."

He waited until Katie was deep into her deep-dish apple

pie before getting to Emily. "Something you said . . . about how you've had two unsuccessful suicides, one successful one, and—what was it?—a kleptomaniac, an arsonist, and these girls who don't eat, and then the other ones who throw up their food."

"Do you know what I call her?" Katie asked impatiently.

"Call whom?"

"My field hockey coach. The one who keeps telling me I'm obese and forbids me water."

"No," David said quietly. "What do you call her?"

"Earth Pig!" Katie exclaimed gleefully. "I started it, and now it's spread like wildfire through the whole school. I mean not to her face, obviously. But I started it." Katie looked grim but proud. "Believe you me, there's nothing more powerful than a nickname whose time has come."

Earth Pig.

David nodded, but his mind was elsewhere, rummaging through a pocket diary in Emily's room, a list of names. Something that Katie had said back at the dormitory . . . Something, something, something.

"And really," he asked her calmly, "you really have an arsonist in your midst?"

"Midst" didn't ring quite true to his ear; it sounded archaic.

"Yeah," Katie said, linking up with him after her Earth Pig digression. "That arsonist is a very sick person."

"She sure is," David agreed. His voice sounded to him almost soothing.

"So far it's been only fires in trash cans, thank God."

He didn't know exactly how he would phrase it; that was the thing. It had to have just the right phrasing or Katie was gone. Actually, the best answer she could give him at this point was a look of disgust. A kind of Earth Pig himself, for daring to think low enough.

"I honestly think that girl should be expelled when they find her. Now you're talking danger. That new dormitory would go up like kindling wood."

"If in fact it's one of the girls," David allowed. "It could be a handyman or a janitor."

"Sure," Katie agreed. "I'm not ruling out anyone."

It was just a hunch, just throwing it into the air, amid obesity and field hockey and medieval prep school life—all the arsonists and kleptomaniacs and anorexics and Earth Pigs that you might bump into upon the greensward at your average prep school. Deep in apple pie and ice cream.

Lingered sultrily.

Quickly now: "There's Emily, but who're the other prostitutes?"

"Well, there's Liz—"

David said quietly, "Oh, yes, that girl we met at the dormitory." He closed his eyes. He felt as if he had been hit.

Katie Owings stabbed savagely at her ice cream.

"How does it work? I wonder."

"I talk too much," Katie muttered, shaking her head as she extracted her spoon.

"An isolated school like this," David said softly, reasonably. "It's hard to figure."

"Hey, are you all right?" Katie asked, looking alarmed. "Gosh, you look as if you've seen a ghost."

"Yes, I'm fine. It's a shock, that's all."

Katie left her spoon sitting up in her ice cream and leaned

against the back of the booth. "Yeah, it takes a lot to make me stop eating." She blew out a long breath.

"Where would they find the opportunity? To do that kind of thing, I mean."

"How did you know?"

"I just wanted to take the worst possibility and work my way back."

"There's a house run by a woman. It's near here. So I understand."

"You don't know?"

"They don't confide in me. It's a little coterie they have. I am not a member."

"But you know about it?"

"It's the school scandal. Most of the girls know about it."

"What about the headmistress?"

"Dunno. She's mainly a fund raiser. She gets worked up about smoking and drugs. Those are her pet things. Do you know what she said in assembly yesterday?"

"No."

"Smoking stunts your growth." Katie shook her head and grimaced. "This is the Ice Age, I'm telling you."

"Why do you suppose Emily got involved in something like this?"

"You tell me, David. How the hell would I know? You're her brother."

"I have no idea," David said. "Have you spoken to her about it?"

"Yeah, I told her it was disgusting," Katie said. "Worse, I told her it was unbelievably tacky."

"What did she say?"

"She told me to mind my own business, and she said what would a fat lesbian know about anything, anyway. This is my *best friend* talking to me. I am not a lesbian, by the way. Just for the record."

"What did you say?"

"Nothing. I guess it's like your story about the Mormon kid and the black sergeant. Emily's in a whole other world. What can you say?"

"Nothing, I guess."

"Anyway, that phase is over," Katie said. "Maybe she didn't like the hours. Now she's entered what I call her Angelic Serenity phase."

"How does her Angelic Serenity phase go?"

"Lots of smiling, lots of radiance, lots of looking on the bright side. The Song of Emily. Next she'll be having visions. None of that is my style. Frankly, I liked her better as a tramp."

"Can I ask you this: Are you still friends?"

"Oh, sure," Katie told him. "I bond for life. At the moment everything's just too huggy for words. I feel as if I'm being slathered with kindness. Forgive the food analogy. You see, David, I'm one of life's sidekicks. You know—the car's downstairs."

"I'm sorry?"

"In the movies the sidekick says the car's downstairs."

"Oh, sure. Right."

"Could you explain to me something? Explain to me how a person possessed of looks, brains and supreme athletic ability —to the point of an outright unfairness by God—winds up selling her body at a roadhouse in Virginia? Somebody has to explain that to me. I've known Emily for three years, but nothing prepared me for that. She's always been on the Technicolor side. America's Junior Miss she's not. What is it? Lack of self-esteem? I mean, that's a lot of lack of self-esteem."

"I don't know," David answered honestly. "All I know is that on paper Emily is supposed to be a very happy young woman."

"Well, I can tell you one thing."

"I wish you would, Katie," David said tiredly.

"She didn't turn pro because she needed the money."

David couldn't leave it like that with his sister. Turning pro. He needed to get through to her somehow. If he just tried hard enough, he would be able to recapture something of the kinship that had flickered so briefly.

After dropping off Emily's cheeseburger-stuffed best friend in the parking lot, he went over to Emily's red-brick dormitory. He called up to her room from a phone in the lobby. He watched the steady traffic of bustling girls on their way to class or sports. All of them looked fully equipped to face life head-on.

Emily answered, and David plunged right in and said he wasn't leaving the school until he saw her again. And she said, with a prim sigh—he was being such a bore, really—"You're very persistent." Then wearily, almost icily, "This isn't like you."

"I'm waiting."

She was just above him, in some little room in the upper floors of the imposing edifice. And he felt suddenly that he was being an infuriating hitch in her plans, whatever they were. "You're a big pain in the ass," she said.

Girls came and went across the linoleum of the lobby—the cream of the best families. "I'm not talking on the phone," David said calmly. "When you change your mind, come on down."

"You can wait down there until hell freezes over." She slammed down the phone.

He thought about that over the next hour or so. That phrase, hell freezes over. He kept turning it over in his mind. He had heard someone somewhere use that expression, and he racked his brain until he came up with Adlai Stevenson at the UN a few years ago, telling the Russians he would wait for their answer until hell freezes over. A thaw in relations. Maybe Emily saw him as an implacable adversary, all bundled up.

No, he wouldn't wait until hell froze over, but he would wait awhile. He settled in and watched the ebb and flow of the prep school girls passing by. He wondered about their lives, which seemed so normal . . . Settling into the comfortable leather chair in the lobby, with a view outside to the campus, an eye trained on the door . . . Lookout . . . Stakeout . . . Keeping tabs . . .

Suddenly Emily was beside him, smiling over him, tugging on his jacket. "Boy, you really settle in," she said, with the first friendly words he had heard from her. Her transformation took him completely by surprise. "You got so revved up on the phone"—and then Emily, holding an imaginary telephone and tucking in her chin, did a gruff-voiced male imitation of a David telling her he wasn't leaving until he spoke to her—" 'I'm not leaving until I have a word with you, young lady, blah, blah.' "

David sat up in the chair. "What's the *matter* with you?" he asked.

"Well," Emily sighed, plunking herself down on the arm of the chair. "What can I tell you?" Dramatically putting the back of her hand to her forehead. "I haven't been myself lately." A splendid imitation of their mother on one of those days when any performance beyond reaching for aspirin was simply *de trop.*

"I gathered that," David said. "I had lunch with your friend Katie today."

"Spilled the beans, did she?" Emily asked with a shrug. "You probably kept plying her with cheeseburgers."

David smiled. "As a matter of fact, she did have a couple of cheeseburgers."

"Then she broke down over the french fries," Emily added with a shrewd nod, looking out the window toward the steps of the dormitory. "So," she announced suddenly, with no change in her amiable tone, "how does it feel to have a sister who's a hooker?"

She certainly went right to the point. "It feels a little strange," David said awkwardly.

"Want to go for a walk?" She stood up abruptly. "Let me show you our playing fields." With just a touch of irony.

Emily took his arm as they went down the steps of the dormitory. The building had the formidability of institutions that will be around long after girlish lives have passed through.

She appeared to be almost physically shocked by the force

of the Virginia sunlight that blasted her on the steps. Again, something in Emily's posture reminded David of his mother that day recently when she had made her slow way from house to car.

They reached the bright grass. Acres of fields developed before them. Emily still held on to his arm, leaning heavily upon it. She felt to him like a frail person, with badly bruised bones. David had the feeling that these were the grounds of a hospital, not a prep school.

When he looked over at Emily tears were running down her face thickly, but she seemed heedless of them. Her cheeks were shining. "I haven't made it across here alone for a while," she said, her voice the steadiest thing about her. "It's so exposed. The grass is like a river. Once I crawled on my hands and knees over to that oak tree over there. I was scared of *something* . . . I'm better now, I'm on the mend. All the things that Katie told you about, I don't do anymore." He sensed she was trying to appease him, make herself normal for him. "Let's sit down here, can we, unless you'd like to keep walking."

Her weight was released from him and she sat down under the tree with her legs gathered under her, and looked calm as a picnic, contentedly pensive, except for her tears. She took then for the first time a distracted wipe at her eyes. "Do me a big favor. Would you talk for a while, and then I'll chip in."

"Okay." But he paused, not knowing where to begin—a year of events to choose from—and then said, first thing, "Jane and Allen named their baby after you. Emily."

"Oh," and there was a moment of disbelief or incomprehension, because she added, "Why?"

"I've told you how much your letters meant to me, and I guess some of it rubbed off on Allen, and they decided they liked the name."

"I hope things work out better for her than they have for me." She said this so simply and artlessly, with such a lack of self-pity, that David was momentarily taken aback.

He decided to ignore it. "I've been seeing a lot of Jane lately," David said. "I like her and everything but I'm not sure we have all that much in common. I'm also not sure she's that interested in me."

Emily picked at some grass, let it scatter. "Still in love with Elise?" she asked casually.

"Yes." There, it had got out suddenly into the green air. He was supposed to be clarifying things for Emily as the older brother with the troubled sister. But she had gotten herself into his soul in one question.

"Is she still in love with you?"

"Who knows?" David said, with mounting agitation. "But now she's taken up with this asshole Englishman, who's probably—"

Emily made an incoming sound between her teeth.

"Well, he's all wrong for her," David snapped.

"Why?" Emily asked gently.

"What does he know about baseball?" David asked, suddenly furious. "He wouldn't know Walter O'Malley from Winston Churchill. These goddamn people should stick to cricket and not be allowed on our shores."

He stood up; he was so mad all of a sudden. A softball game mocked him in the distance, and some girls tossed the big white pill around the horn. And he sat back down again, embarrassed, ridiculous, stunned by his outburst.

"Just out of curiosity," Emily said quietly, "who is Walter O'Malley?"

"He's the guy who moved the Brooklyn Dodgers to Los Angeles," David seethed.

"Oh," Emily said with a nod of amused comprehension. "This *must* be serious."

"You know how Elise gets," David continued in a calmer voice. "She takes everything to heart. She thinks Walter O'Malley is the Great Satan."

Emily looked away. "I talk to Elise sometimes."

"I didn't know that," David said, amazed. "What do you talk about?"

"When I was having a bad time a few months ago, I gave her a call. I was feeling lonely, and I wanted to hear a friendly voice . . . She's a lot like me. She's not a bad person like me, but she must have felt very isolated when she first came to Long Island, a new family and everything . . . She always cheers me up. It's like she's . . . she's . . . come through. And I wonder how she did it." She paused. "I guess I also wanted to get the usual gossip about Dad and Chantal."

"You're not a bad person," David said.

"A bad person?" Emily looked bewildered, as if she couldn't remember having said that about herself. "I've done some things I regret, and some were pretty awful, and some of them you know about thanks to my blabbermouth friend." She was cheering up a little bit. "But I'm pretty strong. I'm descended from good Winant stock. It takes a lot to get us down." She made a fist and thrust it out to indicate pioneer spirit. But this merest effort seemed to tire her.

"Are you going to come home?" David asked.

Emily put a hand to her head again. "Sooner or later, obviously, I'll have to," she said quietly, and a wince crossed her face. "I just don't know when yet."

"We could visit Mom together. Which is better than visiting her alone."

"I feel real guilty about that." She seemed to shrink back from him then and leaned heavily against the tree.

"There's nothing to feel guilty about."

"I'm starting to get cold." Emily squinted up into the sun. She folded her arms across her chest. "Are you getting cold?"

"A little," David said, even though it was not cold outside.

She looked intensely at him for a second. "Can you forgive me?" she asked, and he got the impression that for some reason his answer was terribly important to her.

"For what? Emily, you're my sister." He felt unexpectedly moved and turned away from her. He didn't know how he could make it firmer than that.

"I am so sorry about those horses," she said softly, almost in a singsong voice. "That's the thing I regret most."

At the end, walking back to the dormitory, Emily again leaned heavily against David's arm. She seemed relieved when they reached the safety of the dormitory steps. And David kept telling her that all she had to do was call him—anytime—and she kept saying everything was fine, he shouldn't worry—really. She was planning to come home, anyway. And David kept thinking there was something else he ought to say to her—something vital he had neglected—

but he just couldn't find the right words of love and support. He decided it was better to hold your tongue instead of telling someone you love that it's always darkest before the dawn.

The weird thing was that Emily didn't move from the steps —the slightly shifting girl, looking vulnerable in the sunlight. She was still standing there when his car swept along the smooth institutional driveway toward the front gate. She seemed to be watching out for him, as if she could accompany him in spirit safely off the school grounds. And she kept waving to him, with some heroically mustered energy of farewell.

The horses. The horses the horses. Maybe it all started to go wrong with the horses.

It was late at night and he came out of some dream and there was his father standing over him. He remembered distinctly not being shaken, not being approached. Just his father. "David, get your clothes on. There's been an accident."

And these shapes on the Jepson place, appearing in the headlights, fleeing sideways with their sleek shapes like vertical black ice, pawing, raising themselves like a gallant departure in a Western movie, hoofs in the air, then fading into the night. Fragile-looking as bone could be, as fitness could make them, a terrible beauty—that phrase. It seemed ridiculous to David that you could expect these delicate animals to run great races with a man on top, because it seemed to him that their snapping legs could not even bear a saddle.

Skins of maple and dipping branches, fumes of light. Flickers of fire through the trees and then an explosion of flame and the hell of crackling as tons of air got sucked into some airless place in the distance, illuminating the red Jepson mansion seemingly high above the fire, perched on it yet miraculously unscathed. Fields golden like sunset, but poured gold that dripped onto the turf.

Just some images. He remembered the faces of the grooms, excitement and fear, white eyes and peculiar oddments of clothing—boot matched with sneaker, parka over pajamas, some kind of skullcap that seemed an invasion of privacy when caught in the outdoor night.

And all the sounds and gestures men have when soothing terrified horses—walking them, holding them, patting them, whispering to them, beseeching them, calling to them like lovers.

David remembered a space of peace, walking with his father away from the flames and back to their car, when he had thought that was that, they had gotten them all.

The chain-reaction accident began on the Long Island Expressway a half mile away with this absurdly long scream of brakes that was more like the sound a jet plane might make if it had a mile of runway to work with. David even had time for a wince and scrunch of shoulders to await tremendous impacts of metal—that never came. This was followed by another scream and then a quick loud crash, oddly satisfying. But David made no connection with the horses, none at all—poised and alert now, himself like a horse, nostrils flared, as if he could scent the action happening down on that sunken road far away.

"Do you suppose—"

But his father was gone.

No motorists but five horses were killed in the accident,

spooked by the fire, spooked by the necklace of lights, spooked. They had gotten down to the expressway through a gap in the chain-link fence that separated the service road from the expressway itself.

The carnage defied description, which was not just a cliché but one made vivid in reds and shiny blacks, metals and flesh, metals made of flesh and vice versa.

It took the longest time for the police to get there and destroy the two surviving horses; shots at dawn by then; flutters of coat and whisks of tail for the longest time. All you could do was reach down and pat them and say something like There, there.

Smoke behind them from the fire started by Emily's groom; and the curving shine in front of them of backed-up cars as far as he and his father could see.

What had been handy to his father? What oddments of clothing for him to face the runaway night?

His trustworthy banker's costume, that's what: dark blue suit, white shirt, shined black shoes. But minus a necktie. Immensely dignified. He might as easily have been an early commuter, driving in from the Island to get a head start on the business day. You know how you get that buildup on the FDR Drive after seven: how there's a "window" between eight-oh-five and eight-fifteen which, taken at the flood . . .

David remembered distinctly two pistol shots and three times his father in his suit, among the bodies, his face glazed with rage, every so often baring his teeth. Saying—not a mutter at all—most unbankerly:

That fucking bitch.

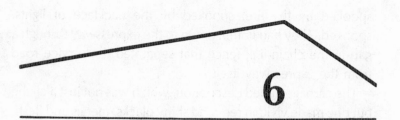

6

The delicatessen was across the street from Jane's apartment. It was run by a small fat lady with a heavy accent who always wore a black sweater and gray slacks. She did most of her business during lunch hour when the men from construction jobs down the street would line up for their sandwiches and beer. The rest of her business was pretty much limited to the small children of the street who bought candy and jostled each other for first place at the counter. They put at least half the bubble gum and chocolate candy into their pockets before they even reached the woman, but she either didn't mind or didn't care.

David felt it would only be a short time before she went out of business. She had an air of great fatigue about her. Sometimes she would sway against the counter, both of her large hands (hands that in some foreign country had perhaps lifted beef or cheese or hay bales) tightening around the edge of the wood countertop.

She recognized Jane and David when she saw them crossing the street and would smile through the window, between the small neon signs advertising beer. She always asked about the baby, then leaned back against the doors of the high cold-drinks case behind her, hands folded placidly, as Jane explained. Nothing about the baby was unexpected; she would nod as if to say, Of course, of course, that's the way it is, but would furrow her brow skeptically if, say, Emily had a cold, and a doctor's advice crept in. David imagined that the woman had had a dozen children, but the only one he had ever seen was her teenage daughter, fashionable and prepared, who helped behind the counter after school and had the same wide country face as her mother.

Above the counter was a rank of curing salamis. Jane surveyed them with a shrewd calculating look while she was waiting for the daughter to cut some meat. Then she moved closer to David and told him that when she was in school the students used to open their lunch pails during breaks, and after a few seconds the cry would go up, "All right, who's got the salami? Who's *got* the salami?" But it was the exact way Jane said it that struck David as so funny; the way she said it being, "Aw'ryyyt, who's god duh salami?"—a long moan and complaint that made the daughter look up from the counter, as if there were a draft in the store. But it was Jane, pacing around as she waited for the woman to wrap the meat. She did once glance at David, who was watching her, nodded to him, then looked away with a haughty sweep of her head.

It was the morning after his return from Virginia. Jane and David left the apartment building and walked up the street toward the park. Jane pushed the carriage, an ancient black vehicle that rocked heavily on its springs. The baby lay in a sea of space, all in white. She was awake but not unhappy; there was a periodic gurgle and flurry of fists.

They walked in silence; an argument between them had not quite surfaced. Jane walked with her eyes straight ahead, chin set, positively sullen, and David beside her waited for her to start it. He did not think it was serious: they would get it over with and have the rest of the day wandering around or just sitting on the grass in the park. It was warm and sunny, and David almost forgot the abandoned cannibalized cars on the street, the overflowing garbage cans.

On the fringes of the park, just inside the high iron fence that surrounded it, two black men were playing basketball, both in sweat suits and sneakers. Jane paused to watch them, as did a small knot of people—not formally watching, but a small group gathered for a moment—for the game was well played. The tallest man, the correct height for a basketball star, dribbled in, smiling at the patter of the other, his back to the basket, which was rickety and had no net. Then the star made his move toward the basket; it would finally be a hook shot, but there was still distance to be covered. His opponent followed him in, closely guarding with both words and body —"Yeah, yeah, *yeah,* come on, come on, okay, okay, *okay,* never happen, never *hap*-pen, never hap— Son—of— a—BITCH—I'll be damned"—sank it with a leap and arc that carried him beyond the basket and left him with a long graceful walk back to his position.

"You didn't like Richard," Jane said, walking on, her face closed to him, voice less angry than disappointed.

"It's not that," David said. "I was glad to have met him."

"Richard has done a great deal for me."

"Okay. I'm sure he has."

"Well, he has."

"I'm with you. What makes you think I didn't like him?"

"Oh, just your attitude." She was busy adjusting the netting over the baby.

Richard had arrived just after David. He did not bother to knock but opened the door, turned and closed it carefully behind him, then stood looking at David and Jane, who were in the kitchen making coffee. Jane said, "Hi, Richard," as if it were perfectly natural that he should stand there watching them, and looked in the cupboard for some cups.

Richard nodded amiably but did not move. He was wearing an enormous brown climber's pack—which David guessed weighed about eighty pounds—tan overalls, a thick wool sweater and calf-high rubber boots. His brown hair, parted neatly in the middle, fell to his shoulders, and a lengthy growth of beard was braided into two thick strands. He had a thin face, and large deep-set blue eyes. He carried the pack lightly, with a slight stoop to his shoulders, and seemed at home in the apartment.

The slime of jealousy crept across David's gentle soul, and the situation ripened.

Jane offered Richard coffee but in the next breath said, "I forgot." He took the pack from his shoulders and set it against the wall. He opened it, removed a plastic jar and metal cup, then busied himself at the stove, oblivious to them. David experienced a minor seething.

Jane and David took their coffee into the living room. In a few minutes Richard came to the door, holding the steamy metal cup. He spoke in a voice so soft that David strained to hear him—a presence at the door but a thin one, almost transparent, with silence a force too, as if he realized that speech was absolutely necessary but it would pollute himself, cup and room. Yet silence would carry him so far but no further.

"Carob, yeast and molasses," he said to David. "Like some?"

"Why not?" David asked ominously.

So Richard had shared breakfast with him, disappearing into the kitchen and returning with different foods—soybeans, boiled wheat, sunflower seeds, rice, mixed and mounded in the middle of David's plate.

"What does he do, anyway?" David asked.

"I think he just moves around," Jane said. "He carries everything he owns in his pack. He rents the apartment upstairs, but he uses it mainly to store food."

"He certainly looks prepared."

"What did you think of him?" she asked.

"I thought he wasn't very interested in what I had to say."

"Well, he has a lot on his mind."

"I know that," David snapped. "But he brought up Vietnam. I wasn't going to bring it up."

"You didn't have to *glare* at him."

"I wasn't glaring at him."

"You were too."

"It was just he seemed so bored," David said, still annoyed. "I mean, if you ask a question like, 'How was it over there?' you should be prepared to listen. I ate his food, didn't I?"

"How noble," Jane replied, exasperated.

"Okay, something went wrong, so what."

"Don't be that way," Jane said. "If maybe you'd gone into less detail and everything hadn't come rushing out; I think that's what turned him off."

"I shouldn't have invited him out to Long Island to see my grenade launcher. I could feel the conversation going down-hill from there."

"I think you expected too much from him."

"Or maybe I'm just a tad oversensitive about this . . . How about right here?"

All of a sudden David felt really depressed about Richard. He was especially pained by his own lack of graciousness. For some reason he had come across as G.I. Joe, which was exactly how he hadn't wanted to sound. Briefly, while talking to Richard, he had posed as someone else, someone strutting and arrogant. He hated this assumed identity and felt deeply embarrassed. Surely that hadn't been him talking.

Jane took the baby out of the carriage and gave her to David. She removed a blanket from the bottom of the carriage and spread it on the grass. The baby was awake, and David playfully held her just off the blanket, soft as putty but with a small wriggling effort to attain footing. There were other couples on the grass nearby, trying to absorb the sun. Jane sat down on the blanket and took the baby from him. She rested back on her knees and looked out across the park.

"I was thinking about Richard and his case," David said. "Is what he said really true?"

She nodded and placed the baby on the blanket.

"It bothered me," David said. "I mean, five years in jail."

"It's not so much that. It's the waiting around that's getting to him. He can't leave the country, not even New York."

"Is there any chance he'll get off?"

"He has good lawyers but it depends a lot on the judge," she said. "There've been so many cases like this; maybe this will be the one that doesn't make it."

The baby started on a long happy crawl toward David, gurgling and curious.

"He thinks he'll just be able to go up and talk to the judge," David said. "I don't think you can do that in a court. You can't just go up and say, 'Well, Judge, I think this is Unconstitutional,' or 'How's your wife?' Can you?"

"He seems to think so," Jane said.

David saw Richard approaching the judge with his full field pack.

The baby grabbed his shoe, ungrabbed it, and looked up at him tentatively. David asked, "When does Emily learn to walk?"

"I'm not sure," Jane smiled.

He picked up the baby and held her over his head; delighted, she waved her legs and arms. "These are the formative weeks."

"David?"

"Jane."

"What's bothering you? I mean, aside from Richard."

"Nothing." He set the baby back down on the blanket. "Why, things have never been better."

She shrugged and said, "All right. Just thought I'd ask." She leaned now on her elbow beside the fringe of blanket. She pulled some grass, looked at it, let it scatter from her hand.

"There's something the matter with my sister," David told her. "The other Emily. She goes to this prep school in Virginia. She doesn't get many weekends anyway, but she's decided not to come home for a while. I went down to see her on Friday, and we talked for a while, but I don't think I really found out what the problem was . . . I guess I'll just wait for her to decide what she wants to do."

"I remember Allen writing me about her and how much she meant to you."

"She used to send me these letters, and I'd let Allen read them," David said. "That's how I got to know her for the first time. Some things she wrote I didn't understand but some passages in those letters were really good. She saw so much about the war I hadn't even noticed. She must have just used her imagination. I'd describe the hills or something, and she'd go off on this long tangent about hills."

Jane put the baby back in the carriage. They had a picnic of wine and cheese on the blanket, pulled from the inner reaches of the carriage, and watched the park lazily, the whole day before them—through the next few hours sleeping sometimes, taking some more wine from paper cups Jane had brought along. Her hands cradled her head, then she leaned her head against David, her hair spread out on his jacket, baby asleep, she just resting there quietly—not a word for a long time, wine-sleepy and relaxed.

So, as casual as the day, between the spaces of the mood that surely would enclose them again, he said, "Would you like to come out to Long Island next weekend?"

"To meet your family?" Jane asked. He sensed the wariness in her voice and knew suddenly that there was going to be a problem where he thought none had existed.

"Well, actually, my father's the only one who's out there," David said. "At the moment. With my mother in the hospital."

"I see." There was a pause but no movement. She did not sit up to look at him. "No, I don't think so, David. Thank you very much for inviting me."

"No?" he asked, surprised. "Why, no?"

"Because I don't want to."

Yes, there was definitely going to be a problem. "I'll have to have a reason, I suppose," David said quietly.

"I've been giving this a lot of thought over the past few weeks, ever since we got . . . involved. And, you know, it seems to me, when you get right down to it, that the only thing we share is Allen. The problem is that Allen's dead. It's taken me a long time to grasp that. But now I have. And I think you helped me."

"Helped you?" he asked, shocked. "I *like* you."

"I hope you'll see what I mean," she said gently. "I've been thinking about it for a while, David . . . and I've decided to go to California after all. I meant to tell you sometime soon, and now I guess this is as good a time as any, since you've asked me to meet your family . . . That was my original plan—California—and I'm sticking to it," she continued firmly. "David, this has caused me a lot of anguish."

You're just walking blithely along, enjoying the day, and suddenly you walk right into a wall. David shook his head tiredly.

She said, "I just thought we should get this cleared up before we took another step and regretted it."

"I wouldn't regret it," he said simply.

This was supposed to be a little picnic in the park. What happened?

"I didn't know any other way of putting it, except to tell you straight out."

"This has nothing to do with Richard, does it?" he asked.

"Richard? Christ. Please."

"A weekend in the country I was inviting you on," David said. "I don't see the big deal."

"It *is* a big deal, darn it. I'd just rather not meet your father."

"Okay," he said, still baffled.

"Can we still be friends? I mean long-distance phone calls occasionally? Someone taking an interest?"

"I don't see why not—if you want."

"That's really important to me," Jane said, sounding genuinely relieved.

"I'm not having a good week," David said quietly. "I'd like to take this whole week and pluck it out of my life."

But he had to admire her, grudgingly. She wanted to take her baby and move to California. Just like that. She could do it —change her life, try her luck, pick up stakes. She was not without a certain degree of . . . fortitude . . . possibly. Annoying as that can be when you're on the receiving end. If keeping in touch was the best they could do—well, okay.

And upon reflection over the next couple of empty weeks, he agreed she had a point. It was a conclusion that he had been reluctantly coming to himself. Yes, it was true. Except for the basic attraction, the only thing they had in common was Allen, and Allen was dead.

So now what?

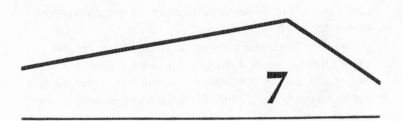

I'm just calling to call, really. I'm out here in Oyster Bay.

Corky and my mother are away for the weekend. Where they are exactly, I can't remember. Hobe Sound probably. Or maybe the boat. Whenever Corky feels like ordering people around, he heads for the boat.

He's thinking of getting a new one, did I tell you that? One with a helicopter launching pad. I don't like the boat very much, but we had terrific times on it. Remember the shark you caught?

I didn't intend to be here this weekend. I had other plans. I didn't intend to call you either, because I think it's your place to call me. You seem to be having a problem with that.

I always feel better when spring training starts. Winter's over. There're only a couple of weeks to go now before they throw out the first ball. I've thought of making the boat my base of operations, park it outside Fort Lauderdale. If I could get Corky's permission, which is extremely doubtful. Do spring training up right just once in my life.

I only got hooked on baseball in the first place to be closer to him. Corky had all this bluster and the game was so Ameri-

can. I wanted to be terribly American more than anything else in the world.

He was a dunce about the game. What a blow. He goes to these sporting events, I think, just to get the animal heat of the crowd. But by the time I realized that it was all for nothing, I could explain the difference between an open and closed stance.

He understood the bottom line but he didn't understand what was going on between the lines. That's pretty good, isn't it?

Anytime a runner gets to third base you should put on the suicide squeeze. Anytime. He honestly believes that, and yet he remains a major figure in the corporate life of this country.

The Yankees are going to be discouraging this year. Don't you feel it in your heart?

Didn't he feel it in his heart?

Don't you feel sometimes that life is like the Cleveland Indians?

I don't mean to sound morbid—gosh, when I start about the Cleveland Indians. But that's the way I get out here. You've always understood about my baseball.

When I'm out here alone I sometimes sit by the phone with the receiver in one hand and my address book in the other, running through names. I'll even call France and talk to my father, which is not so wonderful.

When I get into my car to go back into New York, I always feel as if a tremendous weight has been lifted off me. I can breathe at last.

David had the sensation of falling into his chair, the phone in his hand, like falling into a pillow. The smart thing, instead of talking on the phone, would have been to just drive over to Oyster Bay and see Elise. Oyster Bay was only twenty minutes away.

But he was scared of breaking the connection.

He found his father working in the library; sitting back with his legs crossed, speaking into a Dictaphone. It was an indication of David's flotation that he said, "I'm going over to see Elise now."

His father took off his reading glasses, placed them carefully on the desk, shut off his machine and laid the microphone with equal care beside his glasses.

His father had a certain manner of weighty absorption. It carried over to home from his banking decisions, becoming ironic in the switch. A way of inclining his head, slumping his shoulders against the prop of his elbows, so that he could bring down on the subject at hand the entire raised hammer of his concentration.

"David, are we on the same page?" his father asked gently.

"How do you mean?" He was so eager to be away, to get to Oyster Bay; he shifted from one foot to the other.

"You'll correct me if I'm wrong," his father asked pleasantly, "but once upon a time wasn't there a Jane?"

"Jane's no longer, well, in the picture," David said. "We're still good friends."

David saw Elise going through her address book. *Don't blow it this time,* he thought.

"Son," his father said quietly, with the sepulchral voice he often used on a situation that amused him, "you must be worn to a frazzle." And then he actually smiled and leaned back in his chair.

David paused in his physical and emotional momentum to get going to Oyster Bay. "No," he said. "That's not true." Pausing to take his father's comment seriously. His frazzle. "No. It's the damnedest thing. Everything's fine."

"So now it is Elise . . . again," his father said. For obvious reasons, the prospect did not make him entirely comfortable. Yet he seemed to be bearing up rather well.

"Who knows, Dad? I'm just going over to see her for an hour or so."

His father nodded. "Fine. Now I know the players. I should be finished with all this soon"—waving a weary hand over the papers on his full desk—"and then I'll be going in to see your mother. I should be back in time for supper . . . Marvelous invention, don't you think? The Dictaphone?" His father looked so pleased all of a sudden.

"Marvelous," David agreed.

"Perhaps after dinner tonight we can come in here and play back my voice."

"That would be great," David smiled. "I'm already looking forward to it."

His father raised his hand in blessing.

Except for the two of them, the house was deserted. Through the large window in the living room, he could see sailboats on Long Island Sound.

There was a poolroom with photographs of Corky at his various functions, reunions and tournaments, holding cups, kneeling, standing, shaking hands. And wearing various blazers and sports outfits.

On the wide lawn that sloped down toward the Sound, Corky had erected a netting device that caught golf balls, so he could practice at home. But David imagined Corky aiming for the flags of sails leaning in the distance. Elise said that once Corky after a harsh day on the links had actually teed up and laced into every new ball in his bag. So enraged he kept topping them, and she could still hear the plop in shallow water.

"I don't think you liked to come over here very much," Elise told him. "I feel a little guilty for all those days I used to drag you over. Especially in the summer."

"I loved coming over here," David protested. "I was filled with anticipation."

"You were scared of horseshoe crabs." Elise took his arm.

"That's an exaggeration," David said with a smile.

"Come on, admit it."

"Just because, given a choice of meeting up with a horseshoe crab or not, I chose to stay out of Long Island Sound for my entire childhood, that doesn't mean I was scared of them."

"I thought it was great you were scared of something. That made it more all right to be afraid."

"This is the same girl who once dropped a live horseshoe crab on my lap."

"I was wicked, David," Elise said, with her sultriest, deepest French accent. "I was very wicked."

There was a den with a large television set. David had never seen color television before. Elise swirled like Loretta

Young before his eyes, turned it on with a flick of the knob and said, *Voilà,* extending her hand graciously and balletically for his eyes to travel to the amazing picture.

The magic lantern, Elise whispered, concluding her hostess chores with a little curtsy. This was absurdly erotic.

"My mother is glued to it," she added and seemed with that casual comment to be summing up a life.

The awful squawk of a jingle was between them. She didn't know what to do with her hands; the exquisite TV hostess at a loss. She must have seriously thought that it was in this direction—toward television—that the afternoon would descend.

She was not just in living color; she was there in the flesh.

Everything was quite clear to him. He went over, turned off the television and kissed Elise. She stood with her arms at her sides, then seemed for a moment about to move away from him, to make some movement, when he put his hand lightly on her shoulder. She might have moved from under it but instead remained still and looked at him. She took his hand from her shoulder, held it for a moment with both of hers, then indicated with the slightest nod of her head a vast other room, summed up in that slight nod.

Her bedroom had a view of the Sound. It was surprisingly small and laden with books. One bookcase held French, the other English. Limited space for decoration was completed by two small watercolors of the Seine, a team picture of the '64 Yanks, and, tacked over a small maple desk in one corner, an old bubble gum card of Norm Siebern.

He began to undress her. He kissed her breasts and ran the smooth of his hand along her stomach. She arched back her head and he kissed her neck. Her dark hair fell free behind

her, and he held it up with his hand and let it run along and
through his fingers.

He released her hair and his hand trailed down her back to
her buttocks, along her flank, and she stood close against
him, her head against his chest. He started to unbutton his
shirt and she moved a little away but followed his movements
with her eyes. There was a half light in the room that defeated
curtains, but still he could less see her than feel her next to
him.

Everything was familiar to him—the bed and feeling how
her body tensed slightly when he entered her and then
seemed to stretch out under him. Her head swayed and he
moved back and forth inside her. He felt his own deep sighs
in the room. Her hands curled around his shoulders, first
hinting to him, then tightening, pressing hard against the skin,
grasping him. From a great distance he heard her and felt her
stiffen, and he came in rising gasps that drove him against her.

He felt her hands release him and spread out softly along
his back. They lay for a long moment, and her fingers brushed
him gently. He kissed her and moved off her onto the bed.
She remained motionless for a moment, her legs still open—
David could see her knees in the small light from the window
—then she slowly stretched out her body along the bed.
David reached over and touched her arm. She moved toward him and rested her head against his shoulder. Without a
word he began to smooth back her hair. It gave him great
pleasure to do that small thing.

She snuggled onto his chest with an alarming sense of
security, just as if that were her particular place, well remembered, with the full secure weight of her head.

"How about that," Elise whispered. What made David laugh was the Southern touch she gave it. Expressions emanated from Elise sometimes that apparently had embedded themselves deeply and permanently into her mind, caught as they floated through the air. This was one of her favorites, the signature of a famous New York Yankees radio announcer, conveying something exceptional about the play.

How about that.

When David returned home, he was surprised to find his father sitting in the kitchen alone. Since the servants had been let off Saturday night, David expected them to be there tonight.

His father sat now at the kitchen table, stirring a cup of soup. David came in and asked, "How's Mom?"

His father did not look up. "Feeling better."

"I'll go in and see her tomorrow. Does she need anything?"

"No," his father said. David sensed that it was time for quiet. That was too bad, because he was so happy—happy for the first time in a very long time—and wanted to talk, but his father seemed thoroughly worn out; a contrast to his more upbeat mood of that afternoon. His father looked as if major decisions were on his mind. "There's some more soup if you want it."

"Okay," David said. He went to the stove and put the pan of soup on the burner. He stirred it idly with a spoon, just for something to do. His father was wearing a tweed coat, tie and the gray flannels and shirt of this morning. David didn't want to sit down across from him just yet.

After a minute, his father asked, "What are your plans, David? For the future, I mean."

David shrugged. "Probably finish college"—he paused, thinking of Elise—"maybe at Columbia. I might even try Harvard again, if they'll take me. I haven't made up my mind what I'll do after that. I just can't see that far ahead. Why do you ask?"

"Frankly, it did seem to me for a while there that you were drifting," his father said. "I'm glad you have some plans. It's always better to have a degree." David came over with his soup and sat down at the table. "I guess you've been through quite a lot this last year. I don't think I realized quite how much. It's hard to believe that your own son has been through a war."

"Some good things happened," David said. "I just would have done things differently, like not joining the Army."

They were quiet then. David suddenly felt hungry, got up and opened the refrigerator. He found a large wooden bowl of salad, took it out and put it on the kitchen table. He went to one of the cupboards and removed a glass salad plate. He returned to the table and sat down again across from his father. He could feel his father's eyes on him as he ate.

It was a minute before his father said quietly, "I think you should know that I have decided to sell this house."

David looked up. "You're joking."

"I am thinking seriously of buying an apartment in New York," his father said.

"What made you decide that?" David asked.

"For one thing, I'll be closer to your mother. For another, I don't want to live here alone. Now that both my children are grown and capable of taking care of themselves, there's no sense really in keeping it up. Emily doesn't want to come home anymore, and you will probably be living in the city or Cambridge." His father rubbed his eyes tiredly. "It's just as well, really. I don't see it becoming any less expensive to run. The property taxes alone are thirty thousand dollars a year. Of course, I hope they don't tear it down."

"Tear it down?" David asked.

His father smiled. "I fear it's the land they will want, lad. Perhaps we have held the hill long enough. It's time to give way."

David waited until his father had gone upstairs to bed, then he went into the library. He sat in his father's chair by the telephone for a long time, then he picked up the phone and called Emily's school. He had to tell Emily the extraordinary news. There would be no more home.

A recorded female voice told him that the switchboard shut down after five o'clock on weekends; please record any messages after the sound of the tone, and they will be relayed when the switchboard reopens at nine o'clock on Monday morning. Silence, and David couldn't think of anything to say. "Thank you," the female voice said, and then there was a click.

He thought about calling information, obtaining the school's private number. He had the idea that he and Emily would talk for hours, and he would go down to the school next weekend and they would go out for lunch to some quiet place and discuss last year, next year, school, Elise, family . . .

He stood up finally, with a tiredness that reminded him of other nights walking down roads and narrow paths. The same fear that the next step would bring a flash of light, an explosion—so quick that he wouldn't be able to get out of the way.

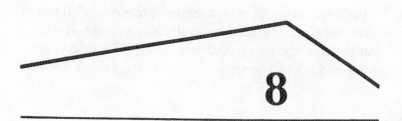

8

In the morning the sound of his father's shower awakened him. The day before him, the past evening, made him close his eyes again. Then he heard the telephone: his father would be the only person to answer it. David nestled back under the covers and waited for his father.

His father opened the door quietly. David lay on his back, his eyes half open, and watched him. His father was dressed in his business suit of dark blue. David could see the vest, the gold watch chain across it.

His father stood for a moment at the bureau beside the door. He looked deep in thought. Then he walked over to the window and pulled up the shade. He announced in a loud voice, "Up, lad. Another morning." He walked to the other window and pulled up its shades. Dusty light fell across David's bed, and David blinked a few times and groaned.

At the window his father recited—gazing out over the driveway—"Your spring and your day are wasted in play, your winter and night in disguise."

His father added quietly, "Blake. Are you ready to greet the morning, son?"

David said, "I'm awake."

"Then cold water won't be necessary?"

"Has it ever been necessary?"

"No, but one of these mornings—splash. Just wait until all that Army training wears off for good."

His father remained at the window. He had both hands in the side pockets of his suit; only the thumb was visible over the edge. There was a scent in the room of his cologne. He grimaced once, and a muscle pushed against his cheek, as if he had seen something out of place through the window. David sat up in bed, arranging the pillows behind him.

His father turned to him and said, with a certain briskness even, as if he wanted to get on with it, "Well, then, something unpleasant has happened."

David would remember his father's erect posture. He didn't know when he had first realized that something was terribly wrong. Perhaps when his father quoted Blake; perhaps when he pulled up the shade.

"Is it Mom?" David asked.

His father shook his head. "It would appear that your sister has removed herself from life."

"She's *what?*"

"Yes, well. It would appear that your sister has removed herself from life."

"She committed suicide," David said. "Isn't that what you mean?"

"To be blunt."

David felt quite calm, really. He thought that *removed*

herself from life was a bizarre way of putting it, but ever so typical of his father.

His father was talking, but David was filled with his sister—all kinds of run-on images. He saw Emily flying through the air. He saw her standing in the middle of a vaulted room. He saw her in photographs, pulling out of someone's grasp.

He thought, very nearly aloud, *This will be over soon.*

"Did she leave a note or anything?" David asked.

"Oh, yes," his father said, really quite dignified in his splendid suit. "Oh, yes. Yes, she left several. She even left one or two bequests. Apparently she had been contemplating this course of action for some time."

"What happened while I was away?" David asked.

He saw Emily tumbling through the air, over and over, in some endless somersault, never landing.

"There were importunings." His father sat down on the bed beside his son and stared into space.

"Importunings," David said. "What does that word mean?"

"Suppose you look it up," his father snapped.

"All right."

But David thought he knew.

"Perhaps I did the wrong thing," his father said distractedly. "I told her it was best if she returned to her school early. I suppose you could say I just threw her out."

Emily lingered sultrily in the front hall, ablaze and vivid in David's mind, and then she was gone.

The first thing David did was call Elise in New York to tell her the news. Doing this was terribly important to him—not just because Elise had been so close to Emily, but because he wanted to be in touch with her. It would have been unthinkable not to let her know. She was the one person in the world that he wanted to talk to.

But at first there was no talking—just a stunned silence from the other end of the phone—for the longest time—and then Elise said finally, softly, "Can I come with you, or would that not be appropriate?"

"To Virginia?" David asked.

"Yes. To Virginia. I would like to come with you," Elise said firmly. "I could meet you at the airport. You just tell me which one. I can be dressed and out this door in five minutes . . . Unless you think it's inappropriate."

"I think it's as appropriate as hell," David said, thinking oddly, *Emily will approve; Emily will really like that.* As if Emily were still among the living. He almost lost control then; he felt the tears fill his eyes, the constriction in his throat. "Let me ask my father, and I'll call you back."

"I'll wait here by the phone," Elise told him. "I would like to be there." She seemed to feel this fact needed extra emphasis, and there was some formality in her voice—making a formal request. "Thank you for calling me, David."

He dressed, went downstairs, heard his father in the library making arrangements for the private plane. He went into the library, sat down—perched really—in a chair across from his father. When his father hung up, David asked him if it was all right if Elise came along to Virginia. He explained that Elise and Emily had been close friends. His father didn't say anything for a moment, didn't appear to hear the question. David repeated it and his father looked at David distractedly, still holding the telephone receiver, almost as if his son's request were coming from long distance, across land lines. "Who?"

"Elise," David said.

His father shrugged. "Yes, quite," and the distracted look did not leave his face.

"Can she come with us?" David repeated.

"Whatever," his father said absently. "I don't mind. Where does she live? We'll swing by."

"It might be easier if she met us at the airport," David said quietly.

"Won't that take her out of her way?" his father asked. He looked puzzled. "I wouldn't want to do that."

This made no sense. "No," David said patiently. "Because you see she's coming with us, Dad, if that's all right. It will be better if she meets us at the airport, I think. That way, we won't have to drive into town, pick her up and drive out to the airport."

"Fine, fine." His father nodded sagely, as if he had given this whole matter grave consideration. "Capital idea."

Finally, his father replaced the phone on its cradle, but it was only when he stood up that he seemed to regain his bearings.

They met in the front hall before driving to the airport. "Let's get on with it then," his father said briskly. The formality of his business suit, the necessity for momentum, seemed to have invested him with a new air of efficiency. He had snapped out of the haze that had briefly afflicted him in the library.

At the Marine Air Terminal, near La Guardia Airport, they sat—the three of them—in a lounge area in a subdued environment filled with businessmen with briefcases. His father leafed through the *Times,* offered Elise the sports section. This struck David—that he would remember that Elise was a baseball fan. Just out of the blue. The airport felt like neutral territory—not his father's house, not the partner's dining room at the bank.

Elise was restless and went off to find a newsstand to buy a magazine. His father pulled out a small blue hardcover book from his comfortably battered briefcase. He donned his reading glasses carefully, meticulously, and began to read Anthony Trollope's *Orley Farm.*

His father's calmness suddenly infuriated David. He wanted to say, "Put that son of a bitch away," meaning poor Trollope.

"What'd she do?" David asked instead, his fingers stained with newsprint. "Jump out a window?"

His father looked over his reading glasses as if David had offered him a suggestion. There was really nothing much in his eyes. It was very hard getting through to him.

David imagined that Chantal Talbot, Elise's mother, got through to him, and that his father confided innermost thoughts to her.

"Pills," his father said.

"Oh . . . I wonder where she got them." Just for something to say.

"What is your thrust?" his father asked, with a tone of mild exasperation.

"My thrust?" David answered. In just a moment he

thought he would have to get up and go outside and get some air. "I don't know if I have a thrust, but I wondered how you felt . . ."

A quartet of businessmen at the next table passed documents back and forth.

His father said nothing. He took off his reading glasses in a flowing motion and let them hang there on his pin-striped knee at the end of his right hand, delicately balanced at the tips of his fingers.

"Importunings," David said. "I looked it up."

His father seemed to weigh the little blue Trollope in his left hand, raising and lowering it slightly. "I didn't see how I could make it any clearer."

"So let me get this straight," David insisted.

"Must we?" his father asked.

"Yes, I think so. As I understand it, Emily made advances toward you, and you rejected them, and then you told her it would be a good idea if she went back to school early."

The businessmen at the next table shared a laugh.

"That is correct."

"You have to understand," David said. "I knew something was wrong. Emily never came home and you never talked about her. I figured there was more to it than just that business about the horses."

"There were other problems as well," his father mused.

"Yes, I know."

His father looked at David with surprise. "Very sordid . . ."

"How did you know?" David asked. "About the prostitution, I mean."

"I received a call from the headmistress a few days ago," his father replied. "At my office. She told me of the problem."

"A friend of hers at the school told me when I was down there."

"Ah," his father said.

Their flight was called over the loudspeaker and David asked, "Why do you think she did it?"

His father shook his head and, without answering, got himself together—the glasses in his coat pocket, the Trollope in the battered briefcase. Elise rejoined them, and David noticed that she had not bought a magazine. Probably, he thought, she just needed to walk around a bit.

His father stood up and moved toward the departure gate. He walked away so fast that David, hurrying to keep up, with Elise beside him, felt a little as if he were pursuing his father with the question.

"Immensely sad," his father said when David and Elise caught up with him. "Immensely sad . . ." Then he went on, under his breath, same two words: immensely sad, immensely sad.

Spring had come to the school, and David was a little surprised. He had expected it to be cold and white. *Sere* was a word his father might have used to describe the place, but in fact the campus was all green. Girls walked around in sports shirts and shorts. The office of the headmistress had a nice view of the playing fields.

It was all conducted with great tact and efficiency, the business of picking up the body of Emily and taking it home. Everybody, from headmistress to coroner, made the process run smoothly. David sensed that his father was greatly relieved by the dignified atmosphere. Perhaps he had anticipated that something intolerable would be expected of him.

Flying home on the same plane, with the coffin in the cargo hold, David asked if they should tell his mother about Emily. His father said, "I have given that matter some thought," very much in bankerly tones. He had decided, "in view of the declining state of her health," that perhaps it would not be a good idea to tell her, "at least not at this time."

"What do you think?" his father asked, turning suddenly in his plane seat.

"Well, I agree," David said.

Thinking about the coffin in the cargo hold, David felt seized by a combination of sadness and frustration. It came over him like a wave. "But how do you *feel?*" he asked his father, in low tones. Elise sat alone on the other side of the aisle, looking out the window. She had been a quiet presence all day, and David suddenly realized that she had scarcely spoken a word since their telephone conversation that morning.

His father looked out the window and said slowly, "I would not like you to think that you have cornered the market on emotion, David. I have asked myself a thousand questions since this morning. A thousand. What should I have done differently? Why didn't I see the warning signs? Why did I throw her out of the house? Why wasn't I more understanding? Why this? Why that? . . . On and on, on and on." His father's voice cracked, and something like a sob filled the cabin of the airplane. "I might have done things differently."

And then it was David's turn to look away. He still held in

his hand the volume of Whitman's *Leaves of Grass,* which was Emily's bequest to him.

At first he hadn't been able to figure out why she had left him Whitman. Then, sitting in that small plane, coffin-laden, he remembered having an argument with Allen in Vietnam long ago. The argument had been about Whitman's hill on Long Island, which David thought was mythical. He must have written Emily about it. How a man could stand atop that hill on Long Island and see shining waters collected in the great distance, north and south.

The next morning the three of them stood in the sunshine by the gravesite at the family plot, with bright lawns falling away. Nothing sere about the cemetery.

The ceremony had a brevity that was merciful, but when his father turned away from the grave, he swayed for a second as if dizzy—as if there were a sudden absence of air—and Elise thought to take his arm. And then David thought to take his father's other arm to steady him.

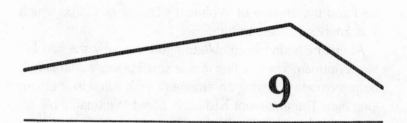

9

It was a week later. David drove over to Oyster Bay to pick up Elise and bring her home for the weekend.

The great thing was that for the first time that week his father had shown more than a little animation. When David asked if it was okay to have Elise over, something came into his father's eyes then, and he said, "Splendid idea." That look was terrific to see, because his father had kept to himself all week. He and David drifted by each other but never really connected. David, locked into his own grief, understood with a pang that his father was very lonely, was looking forward touchingly to company. Now the weekend for him was *filled* —things going on and things to be done.

"I know just the thing," his father added, with a ray of good cheer and an air of mystery that he rather enjoyed wrapping himself in. There was the slightest bustle now to his movements, and David felt relieved to see him so energetic.

"Yes, something mildly diverting," his father mused. "That's the ticket. You and Elise just go on your merry way, and leave everything to me." And then he practically shooed David out the door and over to Oyster Bay.

He and Elise turned into the driveway of his house. David thought of that morning months ago when he had got home from Vietnam. How the car had been stuck in snow, and he and his father had had to walk up the hill.

David went around to the back of the station wagon and took out Elise's small bag. In just the minutes before it grew completely dark there was silence. Last streaks of yellow were overhead, elm branches reached to the border of the driveway, the wings of the house seemed protective.

"Come inside, come inside," his father said. "We can't have me catching cold." He hustled them in, murmuring, "Yes, yes," under his breath, and, oddly, patting the door as he closed it behind him.

It took a little while for his father to relax—well into the cocktail hour. He had to get the players out of the way first. How was Corky? And Chantal? He had to deal with these particular undercurrents of small talk that made him so uncomfortable. Elise's mother and stepfather.

"I have planned a little surprise," his father announced, taking charge of the evening and getting back on his own terms.

They were in the living room, seldom used now. It was the way he looked: in his tweed coat, hands thrust into the side pockets, he was a character he had summoned for the occasion: doddering, blustery, full of good cheer. He actually wrung his hands with anticipation.

"Perhaps nothing so very special," his father said. "But I hope you'll both find it instructive." He turned his full attention to Elise. "I'm trying to turn David into a gentleman. He has been a most reluctant pupil."

Elise smiled. "He's okay the way he is."

"Yes," his father mused, "but there are still a few rough edges." His father looked down at David. "We'll take care of those, won't we, son?"

"Damn right," David said. It was possible that he'd had a scotch too many.

His father sighed and moved toward the door in short rickety steps. " 'An old man in a dry month,' " he murmured.

It was a great supper. The surprise was a wine-tasting. His father came into the kitchen carrying two bottles of wine wrapped in white cloths. He placed them on the kitchen table. He went to the cupboard in the pantry, while Elise and David watched him silently, and fetched three wineglasses. He did it all with such air of ceremony that David almost laughed. He reserved a large crystal glass for himself.

"I'd like to inspect these if you don't mind," David said.

"You don't trust me?" His father looked hurt.

"Sure I do." David inspected the bottles. "Where did you mark them?"

"That settles it," his father said. "Elise will be the judge. We'll turn our backs and Elise will pour it into the glasses. Fair enough, son?"

"Okay, but I think it's fixed."

Elise said, "I promise to be impartial."

"What happened to the old school?" his father asked of the ceiling. "We never had these problems when I was a lad. Honor was honor, trust was trust."

"Wine was wine," David added.

His father turned to Elise. "I'm glad you've taken an interest in him."

They turned away and Elise poured the wine and arranged the glasses. His father said, "This amusing contest is between a Gevry-Chambertin, '57—a bit nutty for my taste. And a Nuits St. Georges, '55—more than a trifle yeasty . . . Now remember which bottle is which, Elise. There must be no confusion."

"All right," she said. "I'll remember." She leaned back in her chair, arms folded.

His father picked up the glass and held it for a moment up to the light. He studied the exquisite play; he brought the glass to his nose. David and Elise watched him. His face seemed to loosen, his eyes closed. He murmured, "The agony of the grape."

He looked at both of them, as if such pleasure were beyond them. He tapped the glass ever so lightly with his finger. He said, "This could only be my old friend Chambertin."

David took a sip from his glass. He leaned back in his chair and said, "This Nuits St. Georges has poetry, yet I sense a conflict."

His father looked concerned. "Conflict, son?"

"It's as if"—David paused—"several of the grapes don't really want it to happen." He looked at his father. "Know what I mean?"

His father cradled his glass for a moment, letting the liquid rejoice against the overhead light of the kitchen, and said, "That is perhaps the difference between a great wine and a very good one."

David nodded. "What the hell, they all hit the spot."

"Oh, yes," his father said gravely. "That is certainly well—if bluntly—put."

David removed the white cloths from around the bottles, and they were both wrong. David had tasted the Gevry-Chambertin, his father the Nuits St. Georges. His father shook his head and said there must have been a mix-up at the bottling plant.

His father conducted the supper with military precision. Elise made a salad, David saw to the vegetables, his father supervised the steak. He gave a lecture on steak from the stove. He checked the salad and vegetables, offering suggestions. Finally his father turned to the old clock on the wall and said, "Now," firmly to himself, and removed the steak from the stove.

David felt exceptionally content, almost glowing, having his own bottle of wine. His face felt red and deep. Periodically he would reach out and touch the bottle, turning it in his hands, as if to check the label.

It was past ten o'clock. His father leaned forward now, with his arm resting on the table, studying his glass. Then he said quietly, "The old man is weary and heavy-laden." David wondered if his father meant this literally. Perhaps, after having marshaled all his considerable energy for the evening, his father was feeling acutely the permanent and tragic absences of his wife and daughter. Even as he sat there with wineglass in hand, some force and propulsion seemed to go out of him before David's very eyes.

At last his father stood up and said tiredly, "What do you two have planned for tomorrow?"

"Nothing that interesting," David said. "I thought we might take a walk."

"Fine. It should be very pretty now," his father said. "The sap rising, and all that. I'll see you at breakfast then."

"Okay," David said.

"Good night, Elise."

"Good night, Mr. Winant," she said quietly. "It was nice to see you again."

His father left. Elise made some coffee. She moved her chair close to David's and they sat for a long while in silence at the kitchen table. They held hands. Elise leaned her head on David's shoulder.

"Let's go to bed," David said.

He awoke just before dawn, and he and Elise talked for a while, softly. At the first light David went to the window and opened the curtain. From the bed they watched the elm trees and sky turn in color from gray to gold.

Elise asked if it would be all right to take a look at Emily's room. David said Sure, but he froze in the doorway as Elise wandered around for a minute or two, lifting a book here, looking at a photograph there, cradling a porcelain figurine, gazing out the window perhaps to see the view that Emily had seen.

And then Elise returned to him in the doorway and kissed him and took his arm, and said, "Okay."

David closed the door behind them. This had been Elise's way of bidding farewell and laying her friend permanently to rest. She was in a brighter mood, with that faithful duty behind her, when they went downstairs for breakfast.

They set off for a walk that morning. It was a clear day, warm but a little windy. David wore a faded yellow windbreaker of his father's, Elise a white sweater and blue jeans. The sweater was baggy and hung down loosely over her hips. Her dark hair was tied with a ribbon at the back.

David thought back to breakfast. His father had sat at the head of the table in a white shirt and dark gray flannels, his face pale and drawn. But he dispensed the Sunday paper with ceremony—"Perhaps the sports section for Elise." Then, as usual, he had driven into the city.

They reached the crest of a hill. Below, at the end of a narrow winding bridle path that cut through the grass, stood a large red barn and silo. It always seemed to David so out-of-place—a building from another century.

Suddenly Elise set off at a run down the hill—out of control and laughing, her arms spread for balance, the tail of black hair bouncing at her neck. She stopped at the bottom beside the barn, breathless, and waved to him.

David walked down the hill and watched her as she made an inspection of the barn. She stood on tiptoes to look through a broken window. She walked around and tugged at the large barn door. She disappeared around the side. A few moments later she appeared inside the barn at the broken window. She shouted, "Hey," and waved to David, looking very satisfied. David came up to her and she said, "You remember all the old carriages they have in here?"

"Sure."

Beside herself. "Come on inside. We'll sit in the stagecoach just like we used to."

And so they sat in one of the stagecoaches from the nineteenth century that evidently Roger Jepson—he of the one-horse sleigh—couldn't bear to part with. It stood right next to the fireman's pumper of faded red and silver, and directly across from the old man's Southern Pacific railway car.

They started with David riding shotgun atop the stagecoach, then moved for a while into the railway car—fixtured, paneled and upholstered just as in its heyday, but layered with dust and cobwebs—and wound up in the passenger compartment of the stagecoach, where of course as a child you had to simulate movement and invent Indians. He and Elise had drifted from one toy to another; and the toys had always been bigger than the children.

As they moved about the barn, David found himself telling Elise everything. He talked to her about Jane, about the war—his nightmares and daymares—about his mother, his father, about Allen. He filled in the last two years. The way Elise listened had a gentleness and sympathy that perhaps came from her own childhood of intense loneliness.

As they continued their walk through fields and along trails, it impressed David how little was left of that part of Long Island in which he had grown up. A couple of fields. A few miles of trails. Several large estates that had already been bought by foundations or historic trusts. There was still old Roger Jepson, though; his enormous red house on the hill, his own railway car a little the worse for wear; and, of course, his sleigh. Apparently Roger Jepson believed that if you can't take it with you, you can at least keep it nearby.

He drove Elise over to Oyster Bay in the early afternoon so she could pick up her car and drive into New York. At her house, David stayed downstairs watching a basketball game on Corky's marvelous color television set, while Elise went up to get her things. When she came down again, they went outside. He found it interesting that when she closed and locked the front door she gave an audible sigh of relief, as if some ordeal had been endured and she were free.

He leaned against her car, waiting for her, looking out to the Sound beyond the house and the running lights of boats and the distant lights of Connecticut. Elise came walking down the flagstone path toward him, holding her suitcase. He had always thought of this in images of her as her saddest pose.

Here she came toward him in reality, holding the suitcase, and really she couldn't have been more full of plans and beans. She was talking all in a rush, as if the house behind her had provoked her to be on a best behavior that was no longer necessary. Tomorrow was Monday and she had classes, but why didn't they have lunch on Tuesday and she could give him the grand tour? That was how Elise put it—the grand tour.

"Sure," David said. "What does that include?"

"My apartment," she whispered shyly. The small suitcase in front of her as if for protection; the world as a foreign hotel. A waif, a wide-eyed innocent, a stranger at life's party—this aura she gave off made him into putty; an effect of which Elise had never been unaware.

"What about lunch?"

Elise shrugged, and made a dismissive deli gesture with her free hand, obviously something common that she had picked up on the naked streets of New York. "So we'll send out."

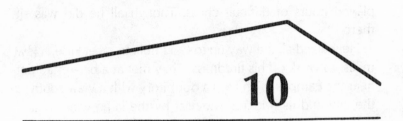

10

He met Elise the next day, after seeing his mother downtown for one of his dutiful visits.

His mother looked really quite well. She had some color but was very weak. When she had her more lucid moments she complained about the hospital and wondered why she couldn't go home. She asked about Emily, and David neatly avoided the topic.

On this visit, before heading up to Columbia to see Elise, he did like presenting his mother with his plans—his college first. It was almost like normality. He probably did this more for himself than for her, because she had no attention span.

There was never anything to do in his mother's room except sit at bedside or gaze out the window down to the East River, which looked surprisingly near and swift-flowing, almost turbulent, running beside the city. It reminded him, without symbolism, that he was on an island.

But always he found these visits with his mother painful and mentally exhausting. Afterward, he felt as though he'd been working on some complex mathematical problem or played hours of difficult chess. Though all he did was sit there.

He walked all the way up to Columbia to meet Elise, a few miles, to work off his tiredness. They met at a bar-restaurant near the campus, high atop a dormitory with a view south to the city and its bridges. They sat by the large window and watched a gathering of lights—like handfuls of lights dropped onto the city—as the afternoon evaporated.

He had a need, like an ache or a pang, to talk to Elise, but not about his family. He dispensed with them promptly. Yes, they did talk about the beribboned bottle of Cristal champagne Emily had left for her father as a going-away present. Which his father had kept turning in his hands almost like a connoisseur.

That bottle had got to his father and put some instant age on him; Emily's bon voyage. It was quite a touch. David had never realized that people could perform their deaths. Katie Owings, his sister's sidekick, had described Emily's final phase as Angelic Serenity.

Elise conveyed her renewed sense of shock and sadness by tugging absently and somewhat comically on the sweater she was wearing. As if she could somehow pull it tighter around her, like a cape. An intense chill had seeped into her. When Elise took his hand hers was cold. "I liked her very much," Elise said.

They had a couple of drinks in front of the living painting of the city and drifted into what they shared. They talked about a week they'd spent on Corky's yacht when they were fourteen. It was the first time they'd slept together. How amazing that Corky and Chantal rarely exchanged more than passing, directional words. Sometimes at meals it was as if David and Elise were the adults with their young civilities, while the adults seemed to be going through a sullen adolescence.

Elise mentioned how Corky seemed to feel that anyone who was his employee must be an idiot for being stupid enough to work for a man like him. This was especially true— or perhaps just more noticeable—within the confines of a boat. Elise knew her Samuel Johnson about boats.

David said he remembered how Corky addressed all the crew members as Stooge. Stooge, do this; Stooge, do that.

God, Elise said, with the traces of utter mortification that would linger forever in her voice, *all we needed was a mutiny off Palm Beach.*

"Funny about your father, isn't it?" Elise asked, out of the blue. "I always wondered why he and my mother never got married. She absolutely adores him."

"I don't know," David said. "Maybe he felt a lot of responsibility to my mother, with all her problems. And maybe to us, too."

"Well, it was really sad to see him all alone the other night," Elise said. "I kept thinking about my mother and Corky. There they are on that horrible boat somewhere off Florida, not saying a word to each other . . . And I just felt really sad."

It might have been just the beer—not Ballantine—but David finally settled down enough to resurrect Emily briefly. He put her in a happier light a couple of years before at a junior tennis tournament at Piping Rock. One shot that he never forgot. A backhand she hit with her feet off the ground, the racquet coming around with such speed and under such pressure that it reminded him of a pulled branch snapping back in place. Feet off the ground, momentarily body-snatched and invaded by the strength of a talented woman. But Emily got worn down in two sets by a chunky girl who lurked in the backcourt hitting deft metronome strokes.

For David and Elise there were prep school dances, exchanges of weekends; all the country clubs and Junior Leagues. They talked a little baseball, a little Yogi Berra in the evening. They talked about her courses at Barnard, and David asked when's the grand tour, and Elise said the grand tour begins tonight if you want to stay over.

But the evening wouldn't have been complete for him if Elise hadn't done her Mel Allen impression. He, the famous New York Yankees sportscaster, with his special signature. This had been bubbling along inside David all day, before the truths of Yogi Berra. That he would finally get to this moment, this safe harbor, which he needed now. But really this need went back to the start of their time together. Before television even, a childhood time.

Perhaps Elise would accompany it with the Ballantine three-ring sign of purity, body and flavor from those dainty fingers. And the little lip-smack that Mel had perfected, which on the lips of Elise always touched deep erotic chords in him.

You had to surprise her with something. It was no fun just asking her. But she wouldn't reveal the abiding truths of America's free airwaves for just any old thing.

How Elise leaned in to talk fervently about a new season. How David swept across the panorama of the vast electric city with a lazy wave of his hand. "Look, Elise," he said, guiding her.

Glancing up, following his hand across the vista of lights. "Oh," she said softly. The spring night had taken her by surprise.

David waited contentedly. This never failed.

Wide-eyed then, brimming with the receptiveness to wonder that was Elise's personal signature. Turning back to him.

"How about that?" she asked.

Slow voices in the night.